SLIDE

NORAH McCLINTOCK

ORCA BOOK PUBLISHERS

Library and Archives Canada Cataloguing in Publication

McClintock, Norah, author
Slide / Norah McClintock.
(The seven prequels)

Issued in print and electronic formats.
ISBN 978-1-4598-1167-6 (paperback).—ISBN 978-1-4598-1168-3 (pdf).—
ISBN 978-1-4598-1169-0 (epub)

I. Title.

PS8575.C62S6 2016   jc813'.54   c2016-900494-5
c2016-900495-3

First published in the United States, 2016
Library of Congress Control Number: 2016933641

Summary: In this middle-grade novel, Rennie ends up on a ski trip
with Grandma and stumbles on a murder plot.

*Orca Book Publishers is dedicated to preserving the environment and has
printed this book on Forest Stewardship Council® certified paper.*

Orca Book Publishers gratefully acknowledges the support for its publishing
programs provided by the following agencies: the Government of Canada
through the Canada Book Fund and the Canada Council for the Arts,
and the Province of British Columbia through the BC Arts Council
and the Book Publishing Tax Credit.

Design by Teresa Bubela
Cover photography by Masterfile

ORCA BOOK PUBLISHERS
www.orcabook.com

Printed and bound in Canada.

19 18 17 16 • 4 3 2 1

To the guys. Thanks for this one, fellas.

Slide: *A fall of a mass of rock, earth or snow down a slope; an avalanche or landslide.*

ONE

It happened when the Major was deployed overseas for a month. To be honest, I was glad to see him go. Mr. Hard-Ass. Mr. Military Police. Mr. You-Can't-Put-One-Over-on-Me. Mr. Eyes-in-the-Back-of-His-Freaking-Head. And always angry about something.

Pick up your clothes, Rennie.

Don't slouch, Rennie.

What do you mean, you passed? This is a C. You think a C is okay? What would your mother say?

Only it was always in French. *Toujours en français. Qu'est-ce que ta mère aurait dit?* And the

1

inevitable *You'll thank me one day—Tu me remercieras un jour.*

As soon as Grandma heard about his assignment, she called him and offered to look after me—as if I needed looking after. I was fourteen already, going on fifteen.

"Put him on a plane, André," she said. "I'll meet him at the airport."

But no, that was no good because I might miss a couple of weeks of school, and then look out! Apparently, they have some kind of heat-seeking missile they deploy against kids who deke off school to go visit their grandmothers. Geez, like it was going to make any difference.

So Grandma came to us. She arrived in a taxi with enough luggage for the duration. The Major's plan: she would ride herd on me until the end of term, and then I could go back to Toronto with her.

The Major came out of his bedroom with his bag. His uniform was crisp. His boots were buffed to mirrorlike finishes.

"Make sure he does his homework, Melanie," he said to Grandma with just enough of an accent that you could tell English wasn't his first language. "And look at what he's done. Don't just take his word for it."

Grandma glanced quizzically at me but said nothing.

"No TV or Internet during the week," the Major continued. "I used to give him privileges—*after* he finished his homework—but all that did was encourage a hurried, slap-happy attitude to his schoolwork."

He meant *slapdash*. The Major messed up words all the time. Some people thought it was funny. He didn't.

My ears burned, even though I told myself I didn't care what he said. I looked at Grandma. She smiled pleasantly at the Major and said, "We'll be fine. Won't we, Rennie?"

We followed him to the door and watched him stride to the car waiting for him in the driveway. He stowed his gear in the trunk and climbed in beside the driver without looking back. The car drove away.

Grandma closed the door against the cold. She rubbed her hands together and grinned wickedly.

"We'd better get you packed," she said. "We have a plane to catch."

"A plane? I thought I was supposed to stay here."

"Rennie, darling, your father left me in charge. So what do you say you humor him and let me decide what's best?"

I didn't even have to think about it. "Okay."

TWO

Grandma is a grandma, which means she's old. But practically the only way you'd know how old is by checking out her birthday cakes (she insists on the correct number of candles, and lately the cakes have been lit up like major cities) or by zooming in on her wrinkles with a magnifying glass. There's no Grandpa. He died so long ago that even my mom didn't remember him. But she used to get a dreamy kind of look in her eyes when she told me what she knew about him. It was like she was imagining him, even though she knew him only through old photographs.

No Grandpa meant that Grandma could pretty much do as she wanted. And Grandma wanted to have fun for as long as she could. To make sure she would be able to, she ate properly, exercised regularly, meditated and was a yoga fanatic. So when she said, "We're going skiing," I wasn't surprised—not until she said, "Where is your passport, darling?"

"Passport?"

"I know the perfect place. I was there, oh, I can't tell you how long ago. I used to take your mother there when she was a girl. She was wild about the backcountry." Her eyes lost their focus, and I knew she was thinking about Mom. I felt bad.

"And we need a passport to get to this place?" Right away I'm thinking, The Alps! Grandma used to go every year and have what she always called *a grand time* both on the slopes and après-ski. She always winked when she said that, and my mom used to roll her eyes and say, *No way do we want to hear about that, do we, Rennie?* I always agreed with her because Grandma's visits put her in such a good mood. "So where is it, Grandma? Where are we going?"

Grandma grinned. "You'll see."

Definitely the Alps.

I ran and got my passport from a supposedly locked drawer in the Major's desk. Okay, so it *was* locked, and I just happened to know, after a few hours working at it—okay, many, many, many hours—how to jimmy the lock. By the time I got back to my room with it, a suitcase lay open on my bed, and Grandma was elbow-deep in my underwear drawer.

"Grandma, geez!" She was holding up a couple of pairs of what I had to admit were pretty sad-looking briefs. I grabbed them and shoved them into the bottom of the suitcase.

"You could do with a shopping trip," Grandma said dryly.

If you ask me, I could have done with some privacy. But it was impossible to get mad at Grandma. Besides, she wasn't criticizing—not like the Major did. She was just being Grandma.

She zipped my suitcase. Outside, a car horn tooted.

"That must be our taxi," Grandma said.

"Taxi? What if Dad saw—"

She looked disappointed. "Really, Rennie. Give me a little credit. Besides, your father runs like a Swiss watch. I gave us a ten-minute margin of safety."

* * *

Here's the great thing about traveling with my grandma: She always goes first-class. We checked in at a special counter at the airport. We waited for our flight in a special lounge. We spent our air time in wide, comfortable seats with plenty of legroom in the front part of the airplane. When I flew with the Major, we always ended up where 90 percent of the passengers sit, packed so tightly that you could barely slip a piece of paper between your knees and the back of the seat in front of you.

When we got off the plane, we breezed through border control—don't ask me what Grandma's secret is with that—and were greeted by a man who handed her the keys to a four-wheel-drive rental. Grandma piloted the heavy vehicle over unfamiliar snow-covered roads at knuckle-whitening speed. She sang along to the nasally voice of one of her all-time faves, Bob Dylan. Well over an hour later, she turned off the main road and onto a narrow, winding one that snaked up into the mountains. She made a final turn at a sign that read *Disaster Peak Ski Resort* and coasted to a stop in front of a large, chalet-style ski resort. Oh yeah—Disaster Peak isn't in the Alps. It isn't even in Europe. It's in the eastern Sierra Nevada range in California, good old USA. But hey, it wasn't the army base, and it wasn't school.

My first impression was that the place was quiet. Too quiet. I got the feeling the biggest disaster around here was the resort's lack of paying guests. It turned out I was wrong about that. The place only looked deserted because

Grandma and I had arrived in the middle of the afternoon, when everyone was out skiing. By the time we had unpacked in our adjoining rooms and Grandma had had a cup of tea, people had started drifting back from the slopes. We watched them from the terrace.

"We'd better go and rent our equipment," Grandma said. "I want to hit the slopes first thing in the morning, if that's okay with you."

We got our gear—and a lecture about staying inbounds and not venturing into the backcountry, certainly not without a guide, because of the danger of avalanches. A person could get killed, the man behind the counter said. People did get killed, just about every year.

"I thought you said you brought Mom here because she loved the backcountry," I said. "Did they have avalanches here back then too?"

"I made sure she knew what she was doing and didn't take any chances," Grandma said. "I expect the same from you."

* * *

We ate dinner in the chalet's large dining room. There were candles on every table and tablecloths like the one Grandma uses for special occasions. Soft music played in the background. After we had our main course—which was just about the best steak I'd ever had, with a side of fries and (Grandma insisted on it) a big salad—and while I waited for my crème brûlée and Grandma her latte, she fixed me with her steely gray eyes.

"I want you to do something for me, Rennie." She leaned forward a little. "I need your word on it."

Uh-oh. What was going on? Had Grandma tricked me? She'd brought me here—I wasn't going to complain about that; here was definitely better than there—but now it looked like she was going to tell me what she wanted in return. Had she stashed schoolwork in her suitcase? Had she talked to my school principal? Was that it? Had she called him up and said, *I'm taking my grandson out of school for a while. What do you require him to learn in his absence?* She'd say it just like that too, laying it on all aristocratic like she was a grande dame, which is what the Major sometimes called her, only he said it in French and I think it means something slightly different in that language.

"Do you promise, Rennie?"

She hadn't even told me what she wanted yet. I guessed she figured she didn't have to.

"It's not like I have a choice, Grandma."

She reached into a pocket and pulled out a small booklet. I groaned. She handed it to me.

"Read it. Memorize it. I plan to quiz you, young man. And then abide by what's written there."

It wasn't homework after all. Not school homework anyway. It was a list of rules about skiing and ski safety at Disaster Peak and the surrounding area. At least half of the booklet was about avalanches.

"Is that all?" I asked. It would be a breeze. I may hate school—I *do* hate school—but I have a good memory. You have to if you want to keep your stories straight for the Major.

"That's it," Grandma said. "But it's not *all*. I'm serious, Rennie. I want you to read that carefully. And I want you to understand that we're sticking to the established runs. We—*you*—are not to go out-of-bounds. Okay?"

What did she think? That I had a death wish? "Okay. No problem, Grandma. I heard what the man at the rental place said about avalanches."

It was a jackpot answer. Grandma smiled as soon as she heard it. At least, I thought that's why she was smiling. It took a few seconds for me to realize that her mood had nothing to do with me. She was all pink in the face over a long-haired, grizzled old guy who zipped past me without a glance, grabbed one of Grandma's hands and kissed it. Grandma's cheeks went from pink to red, like one of those Disney princesses when the prince or whoever finally gets around to laying one on her. And yeah, I've seen a couple of those movies. Girls like them, and sometimes you have to do what they want. So what?

"Melanie." The old guy let go of her hand. "I saw your name in the register. Why didn't you tell me you were coming?"

"I didn't know you'd be here, Rod. I thought you'd be retired by now."

Rod? I stifled a laugh. Old Rod was taller than average. He looked fit too, kind of what I imagined the Major would look like when he was that age—no gut, arrow-straight posture and enough muscle to handle himself in pretty much any situation. A guy who knew that treating his body right could save his life or someone else's. Maybe it even had. Maybe more than once. Rod wasn't bad-looking either. Shaggy hair, more white than gray, but it looked okay on him. Shaggier white eyebrows, the old-man kind that fly out in all directions. Blue eyes that looked like patches of sky between the snowy eyebrows above and the snowy mustache below.

Rod laughed. "Me? Retire? And do what?" His eyes changed, and he looked all mushy when he stared at Grandma. "You look fantastic, Melanie," he said.

"As do you," Grandma said. "Rod, this is my grandson, Rennie. Rennie, this is Rod Billingsley, an old friend. He owns this resort. His father built it."

Rod peeled his adoring gaze off my grandma for just long enough to shake my hand, but by the time he released me, his eyes were on her again.

"Please join us, Rod," she said.

Please don't, I thought.

"I don't want to interrupt your dinner, Melanie. I'm sure you and Rennie came here for quality time alone."

That's the spirit, Rod. Now go away.

"Nonsense," Grandma said. "We're just finishing dessert. Please. Sit. I'd love to catch up, and I'm sure Rennie would be interested in hearing some of your stories."

"Um, actually, Grandma," I said, with a mouth full of crème brûlée, "if it's okay, I was kind of hoping I could take a look around and maybe get some air." Because who wanted to watch some old guy flirt with his grandma if he could avoid it? Who even wanted to think where that could lead? Grandma had a lot of boyfriends—well, men friends. She always did. I heard her say once to Mom…on second thought, never mind what I heard. I don't want to think about that either.

Grandma seemed surprised that I didn't want to hang around and hear some old geezer drone on about the good old days. To Rod, she said, "We've been traveling all day, and boys have a lot of pent-up energy. Or so I've learned." To me, smiling: "You can be excused. And Rennie? You have the key to your room with you, don't you?"

I nodded as I gobbled down the last of the crème brûlée. I could have eaten a bucket of the stuff. "I'll be fine, Grandma. See you in the morning." I got up and kissed her on the cheek.

When I glanced back as I left the dining room, I saw Grandma and Rod leaning in close to one another. Grandma was laughing at something Rod was saying. A lot of things about Grandma were a big mystery to me, but it was no mystery why she had chosen to come to this ski resort.

THREE

Besides the reception area and the dining room, the main floor of the chalet had a large, dimly lit lounge, which was just another name for a bar so you had to be twenty-one to go in, and a slightly smaller family room, full of big comfy chairs and a carpeted space on the floor where little kids could play. The bar was packed. From where I was standing, all the talking and laughing came across as rising and falling waves of noise.

The family room was empty. I headed there. I went to the windows and gazed out at the chalet grounds with their paths and driveways outlined by solar-powered lights. Apart from a man standing in front of a small building across the compound, there was nothing going on out there. In the distance, beyond the compound, slouched mountain peak after peak, like dark shadows rising into the starscape above. I wondered which one was Disaster Peak and how it had gotten its name. Had somebody died up there?

"It's the biggest one," someone said behind me. "But you can't really see it until you go higher."

I shifted my focus so that instead of staring through the glass, I stared at it as if it were a mirror. There was a girl standing in the entrance to the family room. She was alone, so she must have been talking to me. I turned to look directly at her.

She was short but not tiny, just kind of average for a girl. She wasn't so much slim as she was lean and athletic-looking in her tight ski pants and T-shirt. A jacket was draped over one arm. She looked back at me with enormous brown eyes. She had sort of a heart-shaped face, and I think she was wearing lipstick because her lips were a light pink that made me think of candy. Her black hair was pulled back in a long ponytail. She was the kind of girl you saw on TV but never in real life. At least, I never had. She was perfect.

"Disaster Peak," she said. "That's what you were looking for, right?" Her voice was as pretty as she was—like music. I could imagine her singing. I could imagine losing myself in that voice.

"What makes you think that? Are you a mind reader or something?" I know. Not even remotely clever. But I couldn't think of anything except how pretty she was.

"It's what everyone wants to know. Where it is, how high it is and how it got its name." She strolled into the room. "I'm Annie. I work here."

"Are you one of the guides?" Because brother, she could guide me anywhere.

She shook her head.

"Instructor?" I bet she could teach me a thing or two.

"I wish. But no. Think kitchen."

"You're the chef?"

"You're making me feel like a failure."

So, not the chef.

"I wash dishes," she said. "And I don't mind a bit as long as I get to hang around in the mountains and ski in my spare time. Which is exactly what I get to do. What about you? You here with your folks?"

I wanted to say no, because if she worked here and wasn't in school, she had to be a few years older than me, and I didn't want her to figure that out—not right away anyway. I didn't want to tell her that I was here with my grandma either. I don't know why, but it seemed kind of lame. On the other hand, if she worked here— and she did—then she would probably see me with Grandma sooner or later, so what was the point of lying?

It turned out I didn't have to say anything, because a guy appeared. He was tall, with a sun-and-wind-tanned face and sun-bleached blond hair tied back into a ponytail with a strip of leather.

"Hey, Annie." He grinned and ducked his head a little, like he was getting ready to plant a kiss on her. But she elbowed him and nodded at me.

The guy gave me a once-over.

"Yeah, so? You think this squirt's gonna tell on us?" He started to go in for another landing, but Annie pushed him back with both hands.

"First of all, he's not a squirt. He's a guest, and for all you know, he may need a guide, so I'm sure you want to make the best-possible impression, Derek." She turned to me. "Derek works here too. As a guide and ski instructor. Derek, this is…"

Her voice trailed off, and she waited for me to fill in the blank.

"Rennie," I said.

"You ski much, Rennie?" Derek asked.

"I did when we lived in Alberta. And when we lived in Quebec. But where we are now, not so much."

"How old are you?"

I could have said almost fifteen, but he would hear it as fourteen. "What difference does it make?" I said instead.

"Liability, pal," Derek said. "You have to be eighteen to get on some of the slopes around here, and for sure to do any backcountry skiing. You have to sign waivers, and you have to be legal to do it. Mommy and Daddy can't do it for you."

"Leave him alone, Derek." Annie sounded like a big sister standing up to the schoolyard bully. "You're going to scare him." And like I was her baby brother. "Don't listen to him, Rennie. It sounds like you have all the skiing experience you need to have a great time here." She checked her cell phone. "I'm late! Gaston is going to explode. I gotta run." She went up on tiptoe to kiss Derek's cheek, and then she disappeared.

Derek took off. I went outside for a walk. That's how I found out how Disaster Peak got its name. There was a big billboard on the side of one of the buildings, with a map of the area and some history.

The name went back to the 1880s, when a party of pioneers lost their guide after his horse spooked and threw him. They decided to push ahead on their own. They ended up in the Sierras, lost, freezing and starving. It didn't turn into another Donner dinner party or anything. Nobody ate anyone else. They didn't have the chance. An avalanche buried all twenty-seven men, women and children.

Avalanches are a real threat today, the billboard said. *FOR YOUR OWN SAFETY, STAY WITHIN MARKED BOUNDARIES.*

That reminded me of the booklet Grandma had given me. I know the Major thinks I'm a screwup. He's always pissed off at me for something. But I'm not what he thinks. For example, maybe I hate school, but I'm not stupid. And maybe I don't bother with hospital corners— or military corners or whatever; who cares?— when I make my bed, but I'm not a pig, and I do make my bed. Every single day. And yes, I like speed. Who doesn't? But I know to wear a helmet because, like the Major, I'd prefer not to be dead or, worse, brain-dead. So I guess I knew enough to be careful in avalanche country because I for sure didn't want to end up buried under three meters of snow and ice and whatever was in its way before it got to me.

So when I got back to my room, I pulled out the booklet and read it straight through. I have to tell you, if the person who wrote it was trying to scare people, he did a great job. For example:

Avalanches can reach speeds of 80 miles per hour within five seconds.

The deadliest avalanche in American history was in 1910 and killed 96 people.

If a victim can be rescued within 18 minutes, the survival rate is greater than 91 percent. The survival rate drops to 34 percent after 19 minutes. After one hour, only one in three victims buried in an avalanche is found alive. The most common causes of death are suffocation, wounds and hypothermia.

Once the avalanche stops, it settles like concrete. Bodily movement is nearly impossible.

And advice? If you get caught in an avalanche while skiing, you can try to head straight downhill to gather speed and then veer left or right out of the slide path. If you can't get away? Try to grab onto a tree. No tree to grab? Swim. Hard. Why? Because a human body is three times denser than avalanche debris and will sink quickly. Remedy? As the slide slows, clear air space to breathe. Then punch a hand skyward.

I had an even better remedy. Don't go anywhere near an avalanche zone. Being buried alive didn't appeal to me. Not even remotely.

FOUR

True to her word, Grandma poked her head into my room first thing in the morning.

"Rise and shine!" she chirped, striding into my room and throwing back the curtains. I pried open one eye. It was still mostly dark out, but Grandma was already dressed for the slopes.

"I'm going down for breakfast, Rennie. Get dressed and join me. Then we're off for a day of skiing." She beamed at me and mimed shushing down a clear run before letting herself out.

I rolled out of bed. Normally I hate getting up early. But that's because normally my alarm clock is the Major bellowing, *Hurry up! You're going to be late for school!* like he is a drill sergeant and I am a raw recruit. Grandma is a lot nicer in the morning. Plus, she never makes me get up early unless there is a good reason for it and that good reason has something to do with having a good time.

The dining room was full of early birds serving themselves from a buffet table or giving their orders to the cook at the grill behind the buffet. Grandma was seated at a nearby table with a tray in front of her—oatmeal, orange juice, soft-boiled egg, toast, coffee. She waved to me.

The buffet had everything a guy could want for breakfast. I loaded up with two eggs over easy, bacon, sausages, home fries, toast and strawberry jam, orange juice and chocolate milk.

"My goodness," Grandma said. "Well, I guess that answers that."

I took a bite of egg and sausage. It tasted great. I wondered if I could go back for seconds on the sausage.

"Answers what, Grandma?"

"How you got so tall since the last time I saw you. You're almost as tall as your father."

"Maybe I'll end up even taller." That would be sweet. The Major is average in height. That didn't make him any less scary when he wanted to be. But it would be cool to be able to look down at him.

"I wouldn't be surprised." Grandma sipped her juice.

"Was Grandpa tall?"

She thought for a moment. "Yes. He was."

"Because Grand-père isn't." The Major's dad was shorter than the Major. The Major said a lot of Quebecois of his father's generation were short. He said it had to do with their diet. "Maybe I'll take after Mom's side of the family."

Grandma nibbled on her toast. She added milk to her coffee and took a sip.

"How are things going, Rennie?"

I shrugged. How were things ever going? "Okay, I guess."

"And with your father?"

How were things going with the Major? How did things ever go with him? As long as you did what he said, they went fine. If you crossed him or balked, you'd get the trouble you must have been looking for.

"They're okay, I guess."

She studied me for a moment.

"It was an accident, Rennie," she said.

Right. A preventable accident. An accident *I* could have prevented by not hounding my mom to do something she didn't want to do in the first place.

Could have.

But didn't.

The Major knew it. He knew it the minute he found out where it had happened. He put his hands on my shoulders and asked, *What were you doing on that road? Why weren't you on the highway?* He looked at me and knew right away that I was the reason she'd taken that detour. That it never would have happened if it hadn't been for me.

That it was my fault.

I'm sorry, Papa. I'd started to sniffle.

His hands fell away from me. He didn't say a word. He sank into a chair and stared at the wall until a police officer came over to ask me some questions. I don't remember a single one. I was concentrating on holding myself together until I could get out of there. When we eventually got back to the motel room the Major had rented, I got in the shower and stayed there until the Major yelled at me for the third time to get out. It was the only place I could cry.

That was nineteen months ago.

"Your father needs a little more time," Grandma said. "So do you. Now eat up. You're going to need your energy if you plan to keep up with me, young man."

I forced myself to eat even though I'd lost my appetite. The Major had that effect on me.

Rod was waiting for us when we went to pick up our ski equipment.

"I've got a little present for Rennie," he said. He held out a small bundle. "It's an avalanche kit.

I gave one to your mother when she was a girl, except, of course, the technology was different then." He showed me a collapsible probe used for trying to find someone buried by an avalanche, a shovel that snapped together so you could dig and the *pièce de résistance*, an avalanche beacon that could send out a signal if you got buried or receive a signal if you were looking for someone.

"Good heavens," Grandma said when she saw the gear. "You're going to encourage him to stray, Rod. Rennie, you are not to go out-of-bounds. Do you understand?"

"Yes, Grandma." Geez, did she think I wanted to end up as a Popsicle?

"Of course he's not going to go out-of-bounds. But a man should always be prepared up here, Melanie. Isn't that right, Rennie?" He slapped me on the back.

Right. The shuttle to the chairlift was just arriving, so I had no choice but to strap on the gear. I was glad to say goodbye to Rod.

Grandma gazed at the snowy slopes, the rugged mountaintops and the clear blue sky as we rode the lift. She breathed in deeply, squeezed one of my hands and winked. That was her signal that we were going to have fun.

It sure looked promising. The slopes were spectacular! I knew because I'd overheard someone in the dining room say there was a solid base and that a layer of new snow had fallen during the night.

When we got to the top, Grandma scouted out the various trails.

"What are you up for, Rennie?" she asked. "Do you want to start slow, or are you ready for some adventure?"

I have to be careful with Grandma's questions.

"Um, how much adventure, Grandma?"

She had coerced me into cross-country skiing the previous winter. I'd agreed to take the advanced trail because I'd thought, how hard can it be to basically walk on skis? It turned out there was more climbing than walking, the walking was really striding, and there were a lot of tricky downhill parts of the trail that, because of the turns and the obstacles, not to mention the skis, were tougher than I'd expected. I pretty much ate Grandma's snow dust that whole day.

"I was thinking this one would be fun." She pointed to a trail on the large map near the top of the lift: *Devil's Sorrow*.

"Are you sure, Grandma?" Anything that made the devil sorrowful had to be one hell of a trail.

"Of course I'm sure. And if an old lady like me can do it, then so can a strong young man like yourself who is in his fifteenth year."

With that, she pushed off. What else could I do? I followed.

It's a good thing I did. Followed, I mean, instead of led. It meant that I was right there when Grandma took that spectacular fall. I am not kidding—she went literally head over heels before landing with a muffled thud on the snow. She lay there motionless while I covered her with my jacket and went to get help.

FIVE

By the time two ski-patrol guys showed up, Grandma was conscious, but she couldn't walk. I found that out when I tried to help her to her feet. She let out a yelp and sank back to the snow.

"I think I sprained something," she said. Her face had turned gray, like ash.

"Broken," one of the ski-patrol guys said after examining Grandma. "Ankle. I'm afraid you're going to be on crutches for a while, ma'am." He and his partner bundled her in a blanket. He stripped off the jacket I had covered her with and tossed it to me. "You're going to freeze, pal. You have to take care of yourself too. You can't take care of the injured if you put yourself at risk." I zipped my jacket. Easy for him to say. It wasn't his grandma. They secured her to a stretcher and started to make their way slowly down the mountain. I followed.

By the time we got to the bottom, an ambulance was waiting to take Grandma to the nearest town for treatment.

"My purse," she said. "Rennie. I need my purse."

"Don't you worry about that, Melanie," Rod said. He'd been waiting with the ambulance when the ski patrol showed up with Grandma. "Rennie will get it, and we'll follow you into town."

Grandma settled back on the stretcher when she heard that. "Thank you, Rod."

He told me to fetch whatever she wanted, but I stuck around when he asked the paramedics, "How is she?"

"Definitely a broken ankle," one of them said. "And they're going to want to check her over for head injuries. You said she was unconscious for a few minutes, right?" He looked at me. I nodded.

"A couple of minutes. I can't remember how many." It had seemed like forever. I had screamed down another skier, who told me, *No worries. I'll get help.* He was as good as his word. But I couldn't tell you how long it took the ski-patrol guys to get to us either. All I know is that I sat in the snow beside her, saying, *Grandma? Grandma?* over and over to try to wake her up. When she finally opened her eyes, I felt like crying. But I didn't.

"It's a good thing she was wearing a helmet," the other paramedic said.

That was Grandma. She told hair-raising stories about the scrapes she had had as a girl, but she said she'd learned that there was often a hair's breadth between risk-taking and foolhardiness. She said any boy who wanted to survive to be a man should learn the difference between the two.

The ambulance took off, and I ran to Grandma's room to get her purse. It wasn't a typical women's purse. It looked like a courier bag.

That meant I didn't look like an idiot with it slung over my shoulder. Rod was waiting outside in a four-wheel-drive. I climbed in.

For a while we drove in silence, which was fine with me. I was thinking about Grandma. The paramedics said they'd want to check her at the hospital for head injuries. That scared me. What if she had permanent brain damage?

"That paramedic was right. It's a good thing Melanie was wearing a helmet," Rod said without taking his eyes off the road. It was narrow and winding.

I stared straight ahead. He hadn't asked me a question, so I didn't have to say anything. That was good, because I was busy wondering how I would explain to the Major that not only was I not at home and attending school like I was supposed to be, but Grandma had suffered brain damage. For sure he would blame me for that.

Ka-BOOM!!

I jumped so high in the seat of Rod's trusty four-wheel-drive, which itself seemed to have lifted clear off the road for a second or two, that I hit my head against the roof.

"Geez!"

Snow swept down around us, blanketing the sky and covering everything in its chill, white canopy.

"What was that?" My heart pounded in my chest. I glanced at Rod. As far as I could tell, he hadn't reacted. The vehicle hadn't swerved. It hadn't gone even a little off course. It was as if Rod hadn't heard the explosion.

He laughed. I hate when that happens, when someone knows something you don't but instead of telling you, they think it's funny to let you run smack up against it yourself.

"You heard that explosion, right?" I asked.

"I did."

That's all he said. Then more silence. If I wanted to know anything else, I was going to have to ask. It was like with that shrink Grandma and the Major had made me go to every week for a whole year after Mom died. She'd sit there in her leather chair opposite me and say, *How was your week, Rennie?* and then expect me to entertain her by telling her all about it, especially how I *felt* about it (*How did that make you feel, Rennie?*) like feeling stuff was important and I should tell her—a complete stranger, someone who probably wouldn't give me the time of day if she wasn't being paid, which she was—how I was feeling.

Well, forget about that. And forget about games. If you have something to say, say it. Otherwise I don't care. Grandma is the only person who understands that. Mom used to. But Mom was never the kind of person who played stupid mind games. She was a regular person. A nice person. The kind of person you'd enjoy talking to, if you met her, because, no matter what, she would never make you feel bad.

"That was a controlled blast," Rod said finally, shooting a glance at me, maybe wanting to see if I was still alive since I hadn't peppered him with questions. "You know what that is?"

I shook my head.

"I told you this is avalanche country," he said.

Remember that terrific memory of mine? It hadn't failed me. "I know," I said.

"One of the ways we lower the risk of avalanches is by triggering them where we know they're most likely to occur. Or where they happen just about every year."

I couldn't help myself. "What do you use? Dynamite?" It would be so cool be to be the guy who did the blasting.

"There are a lot of different ways to do it. You can throw explosives or lower them onto the site. You can detonate them on the snow surface or above it. You can use a helicopter, or you can use a howitzer or an air gun."

"You have a howitzer? Up here? Who shoots it? You?"

He laughed again. Okay, he didn't have a howitzer.

"I contract with a company that uses a helicopter and explosives to trigger slides."

"So that's what that was?"

He nodded.

We were both quiet after that until we got to the hospital, where Rod took charge. He strode through the main doors ahead of me, straight to the information desk, and asked for Grandma. He led the way to the emergency room, where we found her on a stretcher in a small curtained cubicle. She smiled wanly at us. A guy in a white coat stood beside her. He'd been telling her something when we walked in but stopped and looked at Rod.

"Ah, is this your husband, Mrs. Cole?" He seemed relieved to see Rod.

"It's *Ms.* Cole," Grandma informed him curtly. That let me know that whatever else was wrong with her, there was no brain damage. She was as feisty as ever. I wanted to run to her and hug her. I would have, too, if Rod and that doctor hadn't been in the room. "So if you have something to say about my condition, I suggest you say it directly to me."

The doctor sighed.

"We would like to keep you here at least overnight for observation, Ms. Cole."

"I'm fine," Grandma insisted. But when she tried to sit up, which she did immediately to prove her point to the doctor, she let out a moan and sank back against the thin pillow on the narrow emergency-room gurney.

"You should stay, Grandma." I squeezed her hand. "If it were me, you'd make me stay until you were sure I was okay. I'll stay with you."

Grandma's eyes were closed, and she was breathing a little faster than usual. But she hung tough. "You'll do no such thing, Rennie."

"But Grandma—"

"You're going back with Rod." She opened her eyes and searched the cubicle for him. "You'll take him back with you, won't you, Rod? I'll take a taxi back tomorrow."

"No, you won't," Rod said. "I'm coming to pick you up."

"I want to stay with you, Grandma."

She took my hand in both of hers and smiled. "Go back to the resort with Rod. Have a good time. You deserve it, Rennie. You really do. I'll be back tomorrow."

"Do you want me to call the airline, Grandma? Do you want me to see if we can get tickets home?" I had no idea how to do that, but it couldn't be that hard, could it?

"Home?" Grandma said the word as if she had never heard it before. "Who said anything about going home? We're staying right here."

"But you broke your ankle. You can't ski."

"Then you'll have to do the skiing for both of us. I'll relax in the lounge and drink tea and read a good book—and catch up with Rod." Her eyes twinkled when she looked at him. I guess old people don't look so old to other old people.

"But this is supposed to be a *ski* vacation," I said.

She fixed me with the same look Mom used to give me when she wanted me to pay close attention. It was a look that said, *Mind what I say now, Rennie.*

"Go back with Rod. Have some fun. If you get bored, there's a book in my suitcase. I brought it for you to read. And I'll see you tomorrow. Okay?"

I had no choice.

"Okay, Grandma." I managed to smile even though all I could think was, This vacation is ruined. I felt bad for her.

Rod and I stayed a few more minutes, mostly, it seemed, because Rod wanted to ask Grandma over and over again if there was anything at all that she wanted, anything he could do for her. It was pathetic. We drove back to the resort in silence.

"Tell you what," Rod said when we pulled up behind the chalet. "Annie's off for a few hours after the lunch cleanup. How about I ask her to take you out?"

"Annie who works in the kitchen?"

Rod grinned. "You already met her, huh? I'll talk to her. Your grandma wanted you to have a great ski vacation, and I intend to make sure that's what happens."

Skiing with Annie. Yeah, that would make it great. I could hardly wait.

SIX

Annie swung out of the kitchen a few minutes after Rod went to fetch her.

"Sorry about your gran," she said. "I hope she's going to be okay."

We parted to get our gear and then met outside. Annie chatted happily all the way up on the lift.

"I just love it here. I think when I graduate that I'd like to find a job somewhere around here. It would be cool to live in a small community and to be in the mountains all year round."

"What are you studying?" I asked.

"What *will* I be studying, you mean. I got accepted into premed at Harvard."

I whistled softly. Even I knew how big a deal that was. So not only was she a couple of years older than me, but she was also supersmart. You have to be to get into Harvard.

"What kind of doctor do you want to be?"

"I'm interested in pediatrics. I want to help kids." Her dark eyes sparkled.

"I guess your parents are pretty happy about that, huh?" I said. The Major would probably have a coronary if I managed to do anything even half as good as getting into Harvard.

"My mom died when I was three years old," Annie said. "Cancer."

I didn't know what to do except mumble, "I'm sorry."

"My dad's family wanted him to go back to India and find another wife, but he never did. He died in an accident a few years back. That was really rough. My dad only has one sister. My dad's will made her husband my guardian.

You wouldn't believe how hard I had to fight with him to be allowed to stay over here. I was born here, Rennie. But my uncle wanted me to go back to India. He probably still does. I think he wants to marry me off." She laughed.

"Marry you off?"

"You've heard of arranged marriages, haven't you?"

"Yeah." Sort of. I couldn't remember anything specific about them, just that it was what people did in some countries. No way would I ever go along with something like that, with the Major deciding who I was supposed to spend my life with. He'd probably hitch me to someone in the military so I could keep having orders barked at me, or, as the Major liked to put it, so I wouldn't screw up. If he could find a female drill sergeant my age, he'd have us in front of a priest in two seconds, and anyone who objected would have to face down the Major.

"Most of my cousins have had arranged marriages. My parents had an arranged marriage."

She looked straight ahead. We were halfway to the top. "I remember my mother as being happy. At least, I think I do. Whenever I think about her, I get a warm feeling. I wouldn't get that if she hadn't been happy, would I?"

"I guess it depends on what she was happy about," I said. Maybe Annie remembered her mom being happy because her mom was happy when the two of them were together, like my mom was happy with me. But that didn't mean she had the best marriage in the world.

"Some things we never know because they're unknowable, Rennie." The way she said it, the rhythm, made it sound like something she'd said before, dozens of times, so that now when she said it, it sounded like a chant. She smiled. "And some things are totally knowable, like this. I plan to pick my own husband, thank you very much. I was raised here. I'm not Indian. I mean, I am. But I'm American too. I'm going to Harvard. I'm going to be a doctor here. So there. What about you?"

"What about me what?"

"What do you want to do with your life?"

Geez, what a question. I didn't know what to say. All I wanted was for this part of my life, the part where I lived with the Major, to be over. I wished he'd get shipped out for longer than a month. I wished he had to leave for four years. I could live with Grandma, and by the time he got back I'd be eighteen, old enough to be on my own. That's what I wanted to do with my life. But I couldn't tell her that. It wasn't what she meant.

"I dunno."

"Come on." She elbowed me playfully. "Everyone has an idea of something they'd like to be. It changes sometimes. Like, I wanted to be a nurse when I was a little girl. And then my guidance counselor said, *Why be a nurse when you can be a doctor?* So now I'm going to be a doctor." She turned those enormous brown eyes on me again. That smile, too, and all those perfectly straight teeth.

"I used to want to be a cop," I said. Plainclothes. Undercover would be best. A completely different me.

"Used to? Not anymore?"

"I haven't thought about it lately. Maybe. I dunno."

Lucky for me, the end of the ride was in sight. We both got ready, and I followed her to the slopes.

"My grandma and I went down there." I pointed.

Annie frowned. "That's a tough run for someone...well, no offense, but she *is* your gran."

"Yeah, but she's not like everyone's gran." I liked the way she said the word *gran* instead of *grandma*. "She's athletic. She does yoga every day."

"That ski run and daily yoga are so different from each other that they might as well be on different planets." Annie looked me over critically. "Come on."

She led me to a medium-sized slope that flattened out for a short stretch before falling again.

"I'm going to ski down there." She pointed to the flat part. "You wait here. When I give you the signal, ski to me."

"What for?"

"So I can see how you handle yourself."

"I handle myself great."

"So you say." When I opened my mouth to protest, she said, "Save your breath, Rennie. If I had a dollar for every guy who stretched the truth to try to impress me, I'd be a bazillionnaire. And don't give me that look. Guys do it all the time. I can't explain why. It just is. So do what I tell you, because there's no way the boss asks me to take you skiing and I come back with you broken into tiny pieces because you lied to me about how experienced you are. Okay?"

The *okay* wasn't really a question. Or if it was, she didn't wait for an answer. She skied down the slope and turned to face me. She raised a hand. When she dropped it, signaling me, I pulled down my goggles and pushed off. I was beside her a minute later, still on my feet, nothing broken and, if you ask me, having exhibited some pretty serious skiing skills.

"Not bad," she said solemnly. Then, like the clouds parting and the sun appearing, she grinned. "Pretty good, actually. Let's go."

It's possible I've had a better afternoon at some point in my life and have forgotten about it. It's also possible that I've been King Tut in a previous lifetime and have forgotten about that too.

Annie was a competitive skier. So am I. Not in school maybe, but outside of it. And I don't like to lose. But losing to Annie didn't feel like losing. The fact was, she was a better skier than me. And when she beat me again, she laughed and upped the end point—first with three wins was champ, then first with five wins, then seven.

"First to get to ten wins is the all-time forever champion," Annie said when we'd finished another run. She was leaning on her ski poles, looking completely refreshed, when I reached her at the bottom of the slope. I was sweating and panting.

"I'd have to win the next ten runs in a row to beat you, Annie." I pulled off my tuque and shook my head. Drops of sweat spiraled out from my wet hair and fell to the snow all around me. "I surrender. You're the champ."

"The all-time forever champion," she said.

"The all-time forever champion." I said.

She raised her hands over her head in victory.

"You want to go get some hot chocolate or something?" I asked.

"Sure." She kicked off her skis and ducked into the snack bar. I followed her, and a few minutes later we were drinking pretty good hot chocolate at a table for two. It was perfect.

Until Derek showed up.

He strolled into the café, paused to scan faces and zeroed in right away on Annie, as if he knew she was going to be here. Maybe she'd told him. When he got to our table, he bent and kissed her on the cheek. Then, without even asking, he hooked a chair from the next table, where a man was sitting alone. For all Derek knew, the guy's wife could be about to show up, expecting a place to sit. But the guy didn't complain, so maybe not. Derek positioned his chair between Annie's and mine, closer to hers, and dropped down.

"So, kid," he said. "Did she teach you a thing or two?" He winked at me.

"What's that supposed to mean?" I asked. There was something about Derek that made me want to punch him in the face. He reminded me of Walter, a guy at the school I was in now, which was not the same school I was in last year, but that's what you get when your dad is the Major. You move a lot. Walter was tall and blond like Derek, and he had the same stupid smirk on his face all the time, as if he couldn't believe the lesser beings he had to interact with. I can't stand guys like that.

"He didn't need me to teach him anything," Annie said. She reached across the table to touch my hand. Her skin was so soft, and her fingers felt hot, like they were on fire. "He's good. We spent the whole afternoon racing."

"Is that right?" Derek turned to me. "How many did *you* win, kid?"

What a jerk. I told myself there was nothing I could do about Derek, so there was no point in trying. Just ignore him.

Derek laughed. "Yeah, I've seen that look before. Annie's like a pool shark. You look at her and you figure she wouldn't know the first thing about skiing. Good thing you were smart enough not to put any money on it. You were that smart, right, kid?"

"Rennie," I said through gritted teeth. "My name is Rennie, not *kid*."

"Whatever." He turned to Annie. "I'm taking a party out first thing in the morning. Two days. You think Herr Chef will let you come?"

"What do *you* think?" Annie said.

"Charm him. Bat those gorgeous eyes of yours. Promise him anything."

I couldn't stand the way he looked at her, like he was eating her up with his eyes.

I stood up to leave. I can't prove Derek did anything on purpose, but his foot somehow got tangled up with mine and I tripped. I grabbed an edge of the table to steady myself and ended up tipping the whole table and knocking over my hot chocolate. It fell with a splat onto the floor, just missing Derek's boots.

Annie jumped up and ran to the counter. She returned with a wad of napkins and was about to start mopping up the mess when Derek grabbed the napkins from her and shoved them at me.

"You made the mess. You clean it up," he said.

I'd been planning to help Annie. I'd been about to take the napkins from her myself before he got in the way and grabbed them. He was trying to make me look bad, acting like I was expecting someone else to clean up my mess. But now that he'd shoved the napkins at me? My hands curled into fists automatically. I was itching to hit him.

Annie reached out and took half of the napkins from me. We cleaned up the hot chocolate together, and I carried the sopping mess of napkins to the garbage. I thanked Annie for skiing with me and walked away without a word to Derek. I just wanted to get away from him. I didn't like the way he made me feel, like I was a pesky little kid.

I ate by myself in the dining room. That was okay with me. I took the book Grandma had left for me. Grandma was big on reading, but she never read the stuff that regular people do. She favored big books that were hard to read, which meant mostly books that were written a couple hundred years ago or were Russian. This was no exception. It was a gigantic book of sagas from Iceland. The one I was reading was about a feud that went on for fifty years! At one point, one guy slides by another guy on a bridge made of ice and lops off his head with a sword as he whizzes past. All in all, it wasn't bad, except for all those crazy names I had no idea how to pronounce. After that I went up to my room and watched TV. When I finally decided to go to bed, I looked out the window. It was quiet outside, all black shadows on snow made grayish white from the stars and the moon overhead. It was deserted too, except for two people standing face-to-face beside the equipment-rental hut. A girl and a guy. Annie and Derek. They were kissing. It seemed to go on forever, and when they finally parted, Annie looked up. Maybe I'm crazy, I thought, but I swear she saw me in my window.

SEVEN

Rod was the only person in the dining room when I got up the next morning. Even though I chose a table in the corner, behind a planter, he still managed to scope me out. He came over with his cup of coffee. It turned out he wasn't planning to stay though. He just wanted to tell me he was heading into town later to pick up Grandma and another guest and ask me if I wanted to go with him. It was a tough decision. On the one hand, it was a chance to see how Grandma was. On the other hand, it meant another ride with Rod. And he was bringing Grandma back anyway.

"I think I'll hang out here," I said. "Maybe get a few runs in." Despite what Grandma had said the day before, she might not feel like staying, especially if she was in pain. She might want to go back home to her nice cozy penthouse condo in downtown Toronto. Who could blame her?

"Fair enough," Rod said. He wandered away.

I finished my breakfast, got my gear together and hit the slopes alone. I stayed out all morning. When I finally quit for lunch, Rod was pulling up in front of the chalet. I planted my skis and poles in the snow and hurried over to his truck.

"Grandma!"

Rod had the front passenger door open and was helping her out. She was on crutches, and her face was pale.

"Are you okay, Grandma?"

"Just fine, dear," she said. Her smile was pinched, and there were two little lines cutting into the skin above the bridge of her nose. I knew what that meant.

"You have a headache, don't you, Grandma?"

"Maybe a little. Help me, will you, Rennie?"

I slung the strap of her purse over my shoulder while she positioned her crutches. I steadied her on her feet and stayed close to her as she navigated the path that led to the front door. There was no elevator in the chalet, which meant she had to hobble up the stairs as best she could on her crutches. She made slow progress and apologized for that.

"I'll get better on these things. I have to. The doctor says I'm going to be on them for six weeks at least. After that, he says I'll have to do physio."

When we got to her room, I tried to steer her to the bed. She refused to go.

"I am *not* intending to spend my vacation in bed." She made her way instead to a big armchair near the window. "I just need to rest and let this headache pass. Rennie, be a sweetie, will you, and see if you can scare me up a cup of tea. No milk. A slice of lemon would be perfect."

As if she needed to tell me. I'd been making tea for Grandma since I was five years old. Whenever she'd come to visit, she and Mom had drunk pots of the stuff while they sat at the kitchen table and caught up on each other's lives—and mine. I ran downstairs.

The dining room was deserted. I went to the kitchen door and peeked through the small round window in it. Annie was inside, a white cap on her head like the ones doctors wear when they go into surgery. She was wearing huge rubber gloves that looked like the gauntlets knights in olden times used to wear, except that these were bright yellow and were made of rubber or plastic or something. She was also wearing a huge apron that wrapped almost twice around her slim body and hung almost to her ankles. She turned when I nudged open the door.

"Rennie!" She smiled before glancing around nervously. "You shouldn't be in here. Gaston will freak if he finds a civilian in his kitchen."

"Civilian?" She had to be kidding.

"That's what Gaston calls non-staff. He runs the kitchen like it's an army and he's the general. Or like he's a dictator and we're his minions."

"That doesn't scare me." How could it? I lived with the Major. "My grandma just got back from the hospital. She wants a cup of tea."

Annie peeled off her gloves and went to a small cupboard. When she opened it, I saw that it held a wide assortment of teas.

"What kind does she like?"

"Do you have Earl Grey?"

She held up a packet, waved it triumphantly and flashed me another smile. She bustled around to find a small teapot, a cup and saucer, some sugar and milk.

"She doesn't take milk. She takes lemon," I said.

"No problem." She put back the milk, traversed the kitchen to a huge refrigerator and produced a lemon. She cut a few thin slices and arranged them on a saucer. She filled the teapot with boiling water and set everything on a tray for me. She added a small plate of cookies. "Gaston bakes them fresh every day." She stole a glance at me while she folded a paper napkin into a swan shape and set it beside the teacup. "I saw you last night, Rennie."

Aw, geez. It was like she'd thrown the switch to start my furnace. My face began to feel hot. Then hotter. If there was one thing I could change about myself—besides what happened to my mother—it would be the way I turn red in the face around certain people. Girl people. It was only ever with girls. With guys—with the Major, for example—I had no problem. But girls? Hello, Tomato Face.

"You don't like Derek, do you?" Annie asked.

"I don't like being treated like a kid."

"I don't blame you. I know he acts like a know-it-all sometimes. But he's a nice guy once you get to know him."

Judging from last night, she was getting to know him really well.

We didn't get the chance to discuss Derek's good points because the door to the kitchen swung open, and Rod was standing there.

"Here she is," he announced to the man who was with him, a somber-faced, dark-skinned man wearing an overcoat over a business suit. He had polished city shoes on his feet instead of boots.

"Uncle Raj." There was no joy in Annie's voice. If anything, she seemed stunned by his presence. "You didn't tell me you were coming for a visit."

"Alas, I did not have time." Raj turned to Rod. "I see that my niece is working, but I wonder if you would allow me to steal her away for a few minutes. There is some important family news that I must convey to her."

"No problem. Come on, Rennie. Let's give Annie and her uncle some privacy."

Rod held the door for me so that I could get through with the tray Annie had prepared for Grandma. He headed back to do whatever the owner of a ski resort did all day. I stayed by the door just long enough to hear Raj tell Annie that her gran was very sick and that her dying wish was to see her darling granddaughter again before she died.

I wondered how Annie was handling the news and how close she was to her gran. If someone told me my grandma was dying, I'd be a mess. I'd probably go out and break stuff. I didn't think Annie would do anything so dumb, but she was probably sad. I wanted to stick around and talk to her after her uncle left. But I had Grandma's tea, and it wasn't going to stay hot forever.

Grandma was sitting where I'd left her. Her eyes were closed, but they opened when I came into the room, and she managed a weak little smile.

"Ah," she said. "Is that Earl Grey I smell? I knew I could count on you, Rennie."

I pulled over a small table and set down the tray. I poured her tea, added a slice of lemon and handed it to her. She blew on it and took a tentative sip.

"Oh, that's wonderful. And cookies! Have one, dear." She held out the plate, and I took one. It was delicious, and not just because I was so hungry that a burger at Mickey Dee's would have tasted like a slice of heaven right about then. "I'm just going to sit here and drink my tea and wait for my headache to dissipate. I swear I wouldn't even have it if it hadn't been for that obnoxious man who drove back with us."

"He's Annie's uncle."

Grandma frowned. "Annie?"

"A girl who works in the kitchen."

"Indeed?" Grandma looked me over the way a cop eyeballs a group of kids lurking in the shadows even if they aren't doing anything wrong. "Well," she said, "I hope she has better social skills than her uncle does. That man went on and on about some business venture of his. He had the nerve to question me about my investments! Can you imagine? A complete stranger. I'm pretty sure he wanted me to invest in his business. If you ask me, he sounded rather desperate." She shuddered. "I hope I don't run into him again."

"You probably won't," I said. "He came to take Annie home. Her grandma is sick and wants to see her."

"You seem to know quite a lot about this Annie." Grandma sipped her tea thoughtfully.

My stomach growled like a tiger two days overdue for dinner.

"I have to get something to eat, Grandma." Even if I grabbed the plate of cookies from her and wolfed down the rest of them, I would still be hungry. I needed something substantial. And at this time of day, the only place open around here was the snack bar. "I'll be back in a little while, Grandma. Okay?"

"You run along," Grandma said. "Have some fun. Don't worry about me. I need to get some rest. But we'll have supper together. I promise."

"Are you sure you don't want to go home, Grandma?"

"I'm positive. I brought you here for a good time, and, I must say, you seem to be having one. I wouldn't think of leaving now. Come and give me a kiss before you go."

I did. I'm not a huggy-kissy kind of person. But with Grandma—and Grand-mère—no problem, and I don't care what anyone thinks.

* * *

I got a hot dog and some fries at the snack bar. The sky was the kind of clear blue that was so deep and so, well, blue that you couldn't help but wonder at it. It made me feel good to look at it and to feel the sun on my face even though I was surrounded by mountains of snow. All of a sudden I was glad to be here and eager to get back onto the slopes. I wasn't the only one with the same feelings and the same idea. There was a lineup at the lifts, and I ended up sharing my ride with a twelve-year-old whose parents took him skiing every winter. The kid talked with a funny accent and went to some school in Boston whose name I was supposed to recognize but didn't. I knew from the way he looked at me when he told me the name that it was a big deal and I was supposed to be impressed. It was like Annie telling me she'd been accepted to Harvard, except that when Annie said it, she hadn't been boasting. But this kid? Yeah, he was definitely going for the gusto. So I looked at him like he was a bug, like *if you get too annoying, I'll squash you.* The kid hadn't hit his major growth spurt yet. I had. He shut up.

Skiing with someone was great. I wished that Grandma hadn't broken her ankle and that Annie wasn't going with Derek. Yeah, I knew she was older than me. I got that. But she was fun to be around, and she didn't treat me like I was a pain in the ass the way Derek did.

But skiing alone also had its good points. A guy could think when he was out there by himself. He could get away from everything that was driving him crazy. He didn't have to listen to anyone telling him, *That's not the way you do it, you're not trying, Rennie, you have the brains, I know they're in there somewhere, but you have to apply yourself,* osti!

I didn't head back to the chalet until my stomach was growling again like a grizzly just out of hibernation. I checked in with Grandma, who was wide awake and had more color in her face.

"I just need a quick shower," I told her.

I stripped down in my own room and stayed longer than I should have in the shower because the jet of hot water came out with five times as much force as the water back home, where a shower was more like a drizzle of warm spit. I was getting dressed when I heard the voices outside. One of them was Annie's, which was why I went to the window to take a look. Annie was down there, all right. So was her uncle. They were arguing. Call me an eavesdropper, but I cracked my window so I could listen in.

"I am forbidding it," Raj was saying. Apparently, he didn't care who heard him. "It is enough! You should have come home when your father died. I don't know why I let your grand-mother talk me out of it. A girl your age, you belong with your family and certainly not washing dishes in this…this—"

"It's a resort, Uncle Raj." Annie's voice was calm. If anything, she sounded like she was enjoying his temper tantrum. See? Another reason to like her.

"You are coming home. *Now*."

She laughed. "I'm supposed to be in the kitchen working now."

"Your grandmother would be so ashamed."

"No, she wouldn't. Gran is happy for me. She told me I'd make a great doctor. She wants me to stay here and go to school, Uncle Raj. And you know it."

"You can go to school in India."

Annie shook her head. "I have to get back to work, Uncle Raj. I'm glad to see you, but I'm sorry you came all this way for nothing. I'm not going back with you. Gran will understand. She wants this for me. I know she does."

With that she spun around and disappeared into the kitchen,

I started to close the window but paused when I heard Raj's voice again.

"No, not yet," he said. I snuck another look. He was speaking into a cell phone. "But she will. One way or another, I'll make sure she will." Then silence. When I looked again, he was gone.

"Rennie, are you ready?" Grandma called from the other room.

I pulled on a T-shirt, shoved my feet into my sneakers and went to fetch Grandma.

EIGHT

So there I was, up in the Sierra Nevadas instead of in school, with my grandmother instead of the Major, and with virtually no supervision now that Grandma was confined to crutches and spending her days either at the window in her room or down in the lounge, being fussed over regularly by old Rod. I could do whatever I wanted. Sweet, right?

Pretty much.

I skied all day. I tried every run. I loved that I felt the burn in my quads and my glutes at the end of the day. I went as far as I could without straying out-of-bounds, and then I stood there wondering what it would be like to be over there in the forbidden zone, where anything could happen. Derek did it all the time. He traveled the backcountry, and he guided people through it. He'd never lost anyone to an avalanche, although, according to Annie, he'd rescued a couple of people over the years. I wondered what Derek felt like when he was out there.

When I finished skiing for the day, I stood under the hottest shower I could stand for as long as I could stand it, and I felt better than I had felt in a long time. Being alone, no one nagging at me, no one telling me what to do all the time, getting out there instead of being chained to a desk or *swabbing the barracks*, as the Major liked to say. Just me and the slopes and the sun on my face and all the time in the world. At least, it seemed that way at the time. Even Grandma noticed.

"Perhaps I should break an ankle more often, dear. It seems to agree with you," she said when I met her in the lounge so that we could go into the dining room together. "I haven't seen you look so relaxed in a long time, Rennie. Are you having a good time?"

"I am." It was kind of a surprise how great I felt. "I really am, Grandma."

We took a table near the window so we could look out at the snow that had started to fall only an hour earlier. The flakes were so large and lacy, and the night so calm, that the snow seemed to drift in slow motion to the ground. It gathered on the pine and fir trees outside, turning the chalet property into what my mom would have called *a Christmas-card scene.* I ordered a Coke, Grandma ordered a glass of wine, and we studied the menu.

Grandma closed hers first. Even though I was starving—I seemed to be starving all the time up here—I couldn't decide between the chicken and the steak, both of which came with frites. I didn't know if Gaston made them himself or if some sous chef did, but they were the best frites I've ever had.

"Oh no," Grandma said suddenly. She grabbed her menu, opened it again and started reading it out loud to me.

"Ah, Mrs. Cole," a familiar voice said. It was Annie's uncle Raj. "It is so good to see a friendly face among all these strangers." He beamed at Grandma.

"Oh, it's you, Mr. Choudhry." Grandma's smile was tight, as if it hurt her to even attempt it.

"And this must be the grandson you told me about." He turned to me and flashed his pearly white teeth.

"This is Rennie," Grandma said. "Rennie, this is Mr. Choudhry."

We shook hands. Grandma looked down at her menu. But Raj made no move to go away. He hovered by the table.

"Seeing people together like this, it makes me miss my family. I am not often away from them," he said. "You are very fortunate to have such a fine grandson, Mrs. Cole. You are very fortunate to be able to dine with him, whereas here I am having to dine alone while my late brother-in-law's daughter washes dishes in the kitchen. My dear brother-in-law would be horrified to know that she was doing such a thing." He looked around wistfully before smiling at Grandma again.

A waitress appeared.

"Oh," she said to Mr. Choudhry. "Are you all together? I'll fetch another menu."

Grandma opened her mouth to protest, but for some reason—maybe she felt sorry for Raj— she merely said, "And another place setting. Would you care to join us, Mr. Choudhry?"

"So kind of you," Raj said. "So generous. Yes, thank you. Thank you."

He sat and eagerly studied the menu the waitress handed him.

Raj turned out to be a big talker. He talked about his wife back home and his two daughters, both married to good husbands at great expense to himself. He talked about the sadness that had driven his father to an early grave. Raj was one of three brothers, but he was the only one who was still alive. His other brothers had died a long time ago. Raj had been raising one brother's only son. He was also responsible for his wife's niece Annie.

"I hear you came to take her home," Grandma said. It was the first chance she'd had to get in a word.

Yes, yes, that was certainly his plan, Raj said. But girls these days, especially North American girls, well, they were simply impossible. He loved his brother-in-law, he told us. But the way he had raised his daughter? It was wrong. So wrong. And now here she was, doing menial labor like a servant and refusing to go back home to see her grandmother one last time. "Why is it that you Americans raise your children to be so selfish?" he asked.

"Well, as a Canadian, I'm sure I don't know," Grandma said. She got prickly about her citizenship.

"So you are as mystified as I am," Raj said. "Young people here are so selfish. They place their duty to their families below their own desires and those of their friends. That is not the way I was raised. I was raised to respect my elders. I knew that my parents knew best. Did they not raise me? Did they not, above anyone else, have my best interests at heart? Do parents not know their children's characters better than they do themselves? Do they not know what their children need in order to succeed?"

He went on and on, like a toy with a fresh battery and no Off switch. Even I was glad when Rod stopped by to say hello and Grandma asked him to "join us, *please*, Rod." The *please* sounded desperate to me. Maybe Rod noticed. Maybe that's why he didn't hesitate to pull up a chair and sit down on Grandma's free side.

Before Raj could get started again, Rod asked me and Grandma how our day was. He paid particular attention to Grandma. I wondered if he had been so interested in her way back whenever they'd first known each other. Grandma said it was when they were kids. But I knew Grandma well enough to know that she considered people in their twenties to be kids.

We got halfway through our meal without another Raj monologue and were headed for a pleasant dessert when Rod's face suddenly turned serious and he stood up abruptly.

"Rod, what's—" Grandma began. But he was already striding away from the table and through the dining room.

He marched straight to the entrance, where three men were talking together. Two of them were youngish guys, guests. I'd seen them at the lifts. The other man was older than them. He was wearing a parka with badges on it, like cops have on their parkas. Rod grabbed him by the arm. The man in the parka protested loudly, causing heads to turn in his direction. I guessed Rod didn't want to be the center of attention, because he tugged the man out of the dining room. Maybe the man in the parka resisted. Maybe that's why we heard those angry voices even though it was hard to make out exactly what was being said.

When Rod came back into the dining room, he was alone. He went to the two guests and spoke to them. They didn't look happy. Rod beckoned a waitress, who showed the two to a table and a minute later served them drinks that I bet were "on the house." As Rod made his way back to our table, he was scowling right up to the very last minute. When he reached for his chair, he pasted a smile on his face, but it didn't fool me. I've made myself smile like that too many times. Grandma wasn't fooled either.

"What was that all about?" she asked.

"It was nothing." Rod took a sip of his water and picked up his knife and fork.

"It didn't look like nothing," Grandma said. She watched Rod saw a hunk off the steak on his plate. "It looked like you were angry with that man, the one you strong-armed out of here."

"I'd hardly call it strong-arming," Rod said. He popped the piece of steak into his mouth.

"You made him leave," Grandma said.

"I *invited* him to leave."

Grandma reached for her wine and swirled it in the glass while Rod dug into his baked potato. When she spoke, she directed her words at Raj.

"You probably won't have realized this, Mr. Choudhry, but that man who was invited to leave is a park ranger."

"A park ranger?" Mr. Choudhry looked mystified.

"An employee of the government—either the federal or the state government—whose job it is to take care of publicly owned and designated parklands and wilderness areas. Am I right about that, Rod?"

Rod had just shoved some potato into his mouth. He nodded.

"I could tell from the patches on his parka that he is a park ranger. So my question is—" She looked at me. She looked at Raj. "Why would the owner of a resort in a government-designated wilderness area *invite* a park ranger to leave his business establishment so forcibly? And rather rudely, it seemed to me. Does that seem like nothing to either of you? Because it seemed like *something* to me." She turned her eyes on Rod.

He set down his knife and fork and let out a long sigh.

"You haven't changed one bit," he said to Grandma. "You notice everything. Every damn thing. And then come the questions. *Why are you doing this, Rod? Why did you do that, Rod? Don't lie to me, Rod*—" He broke off abruptly. His cheeks turned pink and then deepened to red. When I looked at Grandma, she was red-faced too. Whatever had happened between her and Rod in the past, it sounded as if it had ended badly. And judging from how Rod had been acting around Grandma ever since we got here, he regretted that. Or he'd seemed to. Now he mostly seemed annoyed.

"I know it's not nothing, Rod," Grandma said firmly. "And I don't like evasive answers."

Boy, could I testify to that! She was like the Major that way. Mom always liked my stories, even if they never quite got around to answering her question. But Grandma? When she asked me something, it didn't matter how I felt about answering it—I knew that sooner or later she was going to get it out of me. She wouldn't leave it alone until she did. I either let her drive me crazy with her questions, or I came up with something that would satisfy her. I guessed Rod knew that too, because he forgot about the steak he'd been tearing apart and he leaned back in his chair.

"His name is Chuck Morrison. He's the ranger around here. At this time of year, it's his job to coordinate avalanche information and make decisions about avalanche control."

"Is he the guy who set off that huge explosion the day Grandma broke her ankle?"

"Explosion?" Mr. Choudhry dropped his fork. "Avalanches?"

"This is avalanche country, Mr. Choudhry," Rod said. "Every guide and operator up here sends regular information to the park ranger. He puts that together with historical patterns and current weather conditions and decides if preventive measures need to be taken. Like a controlled blast."

"A massive explosion," I told Grandma. "You should have heard it! They drop explosives from a helicopter, and it triggers this massive avalanche—"

"A controlled explosion," Rod said, looking at Raj. "It's 100 percent safe provided no one is where they shouldn't be." When Raj looked puzzled again, Rod added, "There are places around here that are out-of-bounds, period. And there are places that are out-of-bounds unless you have an experienced guide or are extremely knowledge-able yourself about avalanche conditions and safety measures. Of course, not everyone respects those guidelines. We get daredevils up here. Young men—they're mostly men, but there have been some young women lately too—who maybe have been somewhere else in avalanche country and have taken a course. Maybe they even have a beacon with them, and a shovel, and the first time they go out, nothing happens. Maybe they go out a second time and still nothing happens. So they don't take the danger seriously. They take stupid risks. They go where they shouldn't go."

"And they get exploded?" Raj looked horrified.

"Well, there's only ever been one incident like that. There have been more incidents of people getting caught in slides."

"Slides?" Raj frowned.

"Avalanches," Rod said.

"And where does that park ranger come into it?" Grandma asked.

"Morrison provides his *expertise*—for a price."

He made it sound like Chuck the Ranger was selling crack cocaine to kids. I didn't get it.

"What's so bad about that?" I asked.

"We get a lot of people up here who want to go off on their own backcountry skiing. They think they can handle it, and they don't want some know-it-all guide telling them what they can and can't do. Chuck encourages them. He gives them a workshop on avalanche safety.

They think it's park-authorized, but it isn't. It's just Chuck on his own, padding his wallet. He sells them maps too, that he claims are based on up-to-the-minute snow conditions."

"Are they?" Grandma asked.

"Are they what?"

"Up-to-the-minute?"

"He prints them off his computer, so I suppose they're reasonably up-to-date," Rod admitted. "But that isn't the point. He has no business encouraging people who shouldn't be out there on their own in the first place. It's a miracle no one has been killed, and all because that man will do anything for money."

"If no one has been killed, what's the big deal?" I asked. Wrong question. Asked of the wrong guy.

Rod went red in the face, which, I guessed, was his all-purpose sign that he was feeling some kind of emotion.

"The point is that he's lying to people. He's telling them that if they follow his map, they'll be fine. He gives them false confidence with an hour-long workshop on avalanche safety. He should know better than that."

"If you feel that way, Rod, why don't you talk to the parks and wilderness people? I'm sure they could put a stop to it."

"I have talked to them. I've written, I've talked, I've emailed, you name it. The problem for a while was that they had no way of checking on what he was doing. He denied everything I said, and since he doesn't keep records, they didn't have any idea who might have used his services. I started keeping a closer eye on some of my guests, the ones who checked in for a night and then disappeared for days or even a week but their car was still parked nearby. I talked to them when they came back, tried to get them to talk. But Chuck was prepared for that. He warned them that I'd probably bother them. He said I didn't like the competition and was trying to shut him down so I would be the only person who could offer access, but at five times the price and with a guide in tow. Nobody would talk. On top of that, I got a reputation as a killjoy.

Chuck's clientele started staying in town while they took his workshop, before they went off on their own. I lost business." He scowled down at the remains of his dinner. "And he still has the nerve to show up here and talk to my guests. I wish I could shut him down."

In the moody silence that followed Rod's explanation, Grandma looked across the table at me. The expression on her face said, *I'm sorry I asked.* Or maybe that's the way I read it because I was thinking, Geez, Grandma, are you glad you asked or what?

Raj took advantage of the silence to tell Grandma all about the business he was developing and how it would revolutionize something or other, blah, blah, blah. Grandma finished her glass of wine and looked at me again. This time she held my eyes as she nodded her head in the direction of the exit. That was my cue to tell her she looked exhausted and that she should rest. "Come on, Grandma, I'm taking you upstairs," I said.

She gave me a huge kiss on one cheek when we got to her door. I had to use soap and water to get the lipstick off.

NINE

I was on a roll, no doubt about it. The next day was the closest I'd ever come to perfection, and that included the past couple of days.

My first clue that something was going my way for a change: When I got down to the dining room that morning, Annie was there. She wasn't in her work clothes. She was in regular clothes, and she was sitting at a table near the kitchen, eating breakfast like a regular person. She looked up when I walked into the room, and she waved at me.

"I was hoping you'd show up. Come and eat with me, Rennie."

My heart did a happy-feet routine. I could feel it dancing and hear the *thumpety-thump* of the drumbeat it was dancing to. She'd been hoping I'd show up! *Hoping.* To see *me.*

I strolled casually to her table, which was an achievement, let me tell you, because my legs felt like cooked spaghetti.

"Grab some food first, Rennie." She flashed me a big smile. "The oatmeal is amazing. You should have some. It's just what a person needs for a day on the slopes."

I hit the buffet and piled stuff on my plate—bacon, eggs, sausage, toast, jam, orange juice and coffee. Plus a bowl of oatmeal sprinkled with brown sugar. I raced back to the table.

"Wow, you sure know how to fuel up," Annie said.

I looked at the debris of her breakfast: the bowl with a few bits of oatmeal sticking to the side, the empty milk glass, the empty plate with toast crumbs on it, the plate with the tiny smear of egg yolk and the splash of congealed sausage fat.

"Look who's talking," I said.

She laughed. "I know how to fuel up too. I have to. Between work shifts, I'm on the slopes. How's your gran?"

"She's okay. She says she's enjoying herself, but this isn't exactly the holiday she planned."

"Do you have to stay with her and keep her company all day?"

"The opposite. She keeps telling me to go and have fun. She *orders* me. I'm not kidding. *I order you to go out there and have fun, Rennie.* That's what she said to me this morning."

"So that's what you're going to do? Go out there?"

"And have fun. Yeah. I have no choice."

"Going with anyone?"

"Right. Like I know anyone up here."

Annie grinned. "You know me. And I just happen to have the day off. And a lunch packed. For two."

That was my second clue. Derek was gone. He was guiding a group of backcountry skiers. But she'd packed a lunch for two. That had to mean—

"I know some great places to ski. You'll have to bring your avalanche pack. You have one, right?"

You'll have to... and she was looking right at me.

"Are you interested, Rennie?"

Was I interested? That was like asking a starving person if he was interested in a snack.

"Sure," I said. Mr. Cool, I hoped.

"Great. Eat your breakfast and meet me outside in ten minutes. And don't forget your avalanche pack."

I don't think I've ever eaten that much food in so short a time as I did that morning. I wolfed down my breakfast and raced outside to meet Annie. I didn't question why she'd said to bring my avalanche pack. I just grabbed it and took it with me.

She was right about knowing great places. They were the least crowded too. After a great couple of hours, she led the way to a small hut where we could sit and eat. She unshouldered her backpack and laid out thick ham-and-cheese sandwiches, a thermos of hot chocolate, apple slices and cups of yogurt.

"Did you really have this packed at breakfast? Or was that what you needed ten minutes to do?" I asked.

"It was packed."

"How did you know you'd run into me?"

"You come to breakfast at the same time every day," she said. She must have been watching me. I felt taller. Older. Better somehow.

"Besides, I was desperate to get away from my uncle." She handed me a sandwich and unwrapped one for herself. "He's driving me crazy. I told him there's no way I'm going home, and that's that. Why would I? My whole life is here. Well, except for my gran. She used to come over and spend a couple of months every year with us when my dad was alive. Did I tell you that?"

If she had, I didn't remember. I wasn't paying that much attention to what she was saying. I was wrapping my mind around what she hadn't said—when she'd needed someone to get away with, she'd chosen me. Sure, if Derek had been around, maybe he'd have been her go-to guy. But he wasn't, which made me it.

"I love my gran. And she loves me. She understands me. I know she would want me to stay here."

"Can't you just call her and talk to her?"

"I would if I could, but she's in hospital somewhere and Uncle Raj won't tell me where. He says she wants to see me in person."

"Someone must know where she is," I said. "There must be someone you can call."

She thought for a moment. Then she took a huge bite of her sandwich.

"Rennie, if it wasn't for you, I'd be having a terrible day. But up here with you, honestly, I think I'm going to forget about Uncle Raj, at least until I see him again. Now eat up. You're going to need your energy for what I have planned this afternoon."

"Does this have anything to do with the avalanche gear?" I asked.

"Yes and no. It's just a precaution. The place I want to show you is safe, as far as anyone knows. But you never know, and I'd rather be safe than sorry. Don't worry. It's not out-of-bounds. It's just that not a lot of people go there. And when I'm not on designated slopes, I don't take any chances."

I said okay because I trusted her. Why wouldn't I?

We had to do a lot of climbing, and I hate to admit it, but I got winded faster than she did. I don't think she got winded at all. But we made it to the top of a run she wanted to take me on, and I still can't believe it, but what I was thinking was, Geez, this is the most beautiful place I've ever seen. It was just rock and snow. And sky. Lots of sky. But it hit me the way a certain Christmas song does, one that my mom used to sing to me, and it made me want to cry. I'd never felt that way about scenery before.

By the time we'd swooped and arced our way across and down and finally made our way back to the chalet again, my stomach was growling.

"Annie, I have an idea," I said. I felt kind of shy about it. "Why don't you have supper with my grandma and me?"

"I wish I could. But there's something I need to do right now, thanks to you, Rennie." Thanks to me? What did I do? "And then I'm going to talk to Uncle Raj and hopefully settle this once and for all." She kissed me on the cheek. "Thanks for a great day. I really needed that."

I was grinning like a fool as I watched her disappear around the back of the chalet.

It took a while for me to get showered and changed and then to help Grandma down the stairs to the dining room. She hesitated at the doorway and surveyed the room.

"I do hope that Mr. Choudhry won't stop by our table again," she said.

"I don't think you have to worry about that, Grandma."

"Oh?"

She followed my gaze to the back of the dining room, where Annie and her uncle sat staring earnestly at each other across a small table. Annie was talking. Raj was leaning forward, listening intently to everything she was saying. The whole time, he was shaking his head. It was almost hypnotizing, watching it tick left, right, left, right.

Annie, unlike her uncle, seemed calmer. She sat straight in her chair, her hands together in her lap, her eyes on her uncle's. When she finished talking, she kept her gaze on him. He was still leaning across the table, but now he was scowling. He tore the cloth napkin off his lap and threw it onto the table. He didn't notice us when he stormed past us on his way out of the dining room. I don't think he noticed anything.

"Well, he certainly doesn't look happy." Grandma didn't sound particularly sympathetic. "I take it that young lady is his niece."

"Do you mind if I talk to her for a minute, Grandma?"

She smiled. "I'll get us a table, shall I?"

Annie hadn't moved. She seemed perfectly content eating her dinner while her uncle's sat untouched across from her.

"Is everything okay, Annie?"

She held up a finger, a signal for me to wait while she swallowed the piece of chicken she'd just popped into her mouth.

"Everything's fine, Rennie. Why?"

"I just saw your uncle. He looked angry."

"That's his problem. When you tell lies, you run the risk of getting caught. And when you get caught, you deserve whatever happens next."

"Your uncle lied to you?"

"You bet he did." She said this to a few bars of some sappy Sarah McLachlan song. It turned out that was her cell-phone ring. "Sorry, Rennie. I have to take this."

I made my way to the table Grandma had chosen. When I looked back at Annie, she was on her way out of the dining room, her cell phone pressed to her ear.

TEN

After Mom died, after the way it happened, after the way I felt and the way I acted, my teacher had talked to my vice-principal, who had called in the Major, who had then taken me to see a child psychologist. Everyone thought I needed help. Everybody told me over and over, *It wasn't your fault, Rennie.* Even the Major said it. They didn't know what they were talking about. They weren't there when it happened. They didn't know what came before.

A child psychologist wasn't what I was expecting. The Major had to drag me there. And I do mean drag. I was hiding out in the bush behind school, and he found me, don't ask me how, and gripped my arm while I kicked and twisted and tried to punch. He finally wrestled me into the car and drove me to one of those low-rise buildings filled with dentists, doctors and optometrists and shrinks. He pretty much pushed me into the guy's office and retreated to the waiting room to, well, to wait.

Hi, I'm Pete. The psychologist—I know psychologists aren't real shrinks, but some of them are as good as—thrust out a hand, sounding and looking like a salesman acting all friendly to clinch a deal. But it turned out Pete was okay. He would lean back in his chair, one arm draped over the back of it, and we would *shoot the shit*, as he liked to put it. He said a lot of things over the time I saw him. He did his best to make me talk too, which I didn't at first. Not about what he wanted me to anyway. But sometimes we talked baseball or basketball—the pros, I mean. One time we debated comics versus the movies based on them.

That kind of stuff. One of the things Pete was big on was this: the only constant in life is change.

Nothing stays the same, Rennie. Not that tree out there, not this building, not you, not the way you feel. Everything changes. Everything is changing all the time. When things get bad, you have to know they won't stay that way forever. They'll eventually get better. You won't always feel exactly the way you feel now.

This is what he didn't say: When things are good, you have to know they won't stay that way forever. They'll eventually turn bad.

Now I'd had a run of excellent days. I couldn't help wondering when that would change. The day started okay. I had a great time on the slopes. I did some runs I hadn't done before, and I met a guy named John who was staying at another resort but was on his own for the day and was a year older than me and knew his way around. We were on our way back because he had to meet his parents for lunch. I was going to check on Grandma, even if she didn't think she needed checking on. When I paused to wait for John to blow his nose and catch up to me, I spotted something nestled way down on the snowy floor of the valley below. A winding road led up to it.

"What's that?" I asked. "Someone's ski cabin?"

"Ranger station." John pulled on his gloves.

A car appeared on the road that led to the ranger station. It stopped when it arrived at the cabin, and a man got out. Even at this distance, I recognized him. It was Raj. There was no mistaking him picking his way through the snow in those shoes of his. They had smooth soles that gave him no traction. He hadn't gone more than a couple of steps before his feet flew out from under him, and I was sure he was going to crash to the ground. He didn't. With a lot of frantic arm and leg movement, he managed to stay upright.

"Are you coming or not?" John asked. "My mom freaks if I'm late—for anything."

We headed back the way we had come, said we would text each other about maybe going out the next day, and I headed for the resort.

I changed and checked in with Grandma only to find that she would be lunching with a "fascinating" woman she'd met earlier that day. They were going to drive into town, Grandma's crutches and all, for a lecture on the history of the Sierra Nevada. They would be back for dinner. Good for Grandma, I thought. It wasn't my idea of a wild time, but it was better than her sitting by herself all day having no fun while I was out skiing and, more important, missing school. I was on my way to the dining room for lunch when I heard a yelp from the back hall, where the staff entrance to the kitchen was. It sounded like Annie. I pictured Raj's face the night before when he had stormed past us, his face twisted in rage. I decided to investigate.

Annie had indeed yelped because someone was pulling her down the hall, away from the kitchen and toward the back door. But it wasn't Raj. It was Derek.

"Derek, no!" Annie howled. She looked serious about it too. She wasn't smiling or fooling around.

"I'm already in trouble with Chef. I suggested some improvements to his chicken tikka—my dad made the best chicken tikka ever—and he's been picking on me ever since. I've washed some dishes five times. He keeps sending them back saying that they're filthy. He makes me stay as long as it takes to get it right. So really, Derek, it's in your best interest to *let go of me.*"

"Annie, have a heart. I just got back." He wrapped one arm around her waist and pulled her close, despite the struggle she was putting up. I felt my whole body tense.

"I have to go. I mean it, Derek!" Annie was doing her best to wriggle free. Her face had turned red.

"Just come outside for a minute. I haven't seen you in ages."

"It's only been two days." With a sudden burst of strength, she broke free. He quickly caught both of her hands and pulled her toward the exit. Derek was a lot bigger than Annie. A lot stronger too. I couldn't take it anymore. I couldn't take *him* anymore.

"You heard what she said, Derek. Let her go." I stepped out from where I'd been watching them.

Derek looked at me, puzzled. Maybe he was wondering where I had come from. Maybe he was wondering what his business had to do with me. He still had a grip on Annie. Slowly his expression changed.

"Were you spying on us, squirt? Or should I say, spying on Annie?"

"Let her go. She doesn't want to go with you." I stepped closer. Yeah, he was taller and older than me, and he was packing more weight, a lot of it muscle. But he didn't scare me. I don't scare that easily.

"Buzz off, fruit fly."

"It's okay, Rennie," Annie said. "I can handle this."

Derek grinned and tried to kiss her on the cheek. She pulled away.

"Derek, I wanted to tell you later, but you're forcing me to tell you now." Her face grew deadly serious. "I talked to my uncle. He's pressure me to go back home."

Derek's face changed too. His smirk vanished. "No way! You can't go back there! You can't let your uncle decide what the rest of your life is going to be like."

"It's the way my family does things, Derek."

I thought I saw a faint smile, but I don't think Derek noticed. "My uncle thinks it's time I got married. I told you about arranged marriages, didn't I, Derek?"

He stared at her in stunned silence. He grabbed her again.

"I won't let you go," he said. "If he gets you over there, you'll never come back. I know it."

"Derek, you're hurting me."

That's when I lost it.

I lunged at Derek. He was ready for me. He raised both hands and shoved me hard in the chest. I staggered backward. By the time I caught my balance, my hands had turned into fists, and all I was thinking was that I don't like being shoved.

I didn't think he was looking when I pulled my right fist back. He had turned back to Annie. I turned out to be wrong.

Before my fist could connect with him, one of his caught me on my left jaw, snapping my head around so fast and so far that I'm surprised my neck didn't twist right off. I reeled backward and landed flat on my butt, dazed and literally seeing stars. I am not kidding.

Arms went around me. Annie's arms.

"Rennie, are you okay?"

"Yeah." I didn't feel okay. My whole head throbbed. Annie helped me to my feet.

"Get out of here, Derek! Just get out of here!"

"Annie, I—"

"Go! Go before you have to explain this."

He skulked away. Annie turned my head gently so that she could inspect me.

"Can you open and close your mouth?" she asked.

I could, but it hurt.

"So at least your jaw isn't broken. But you need ice. Come on." She took me by the hand, and there I was, instantly transported to heaven. That's what it felt like. I wished I was older and could get rid of Derek. I wished a few other things too.

Annie led me back to the staff entrance and into the kitchen, where three men bustled from grill to stove to burner, assembling meals for the guests. One of them scowled and pointed to the clock when Annie came in.

"I'm sorry, Chef," she said. "But one of the guests had an accident." She pointed to my face. "I need ice."

Chef took a look at me and waved her on impatiently.

She steered me to a fridge stocked only with vegetables. There was a drawer at the bottom. She opened it. It was full of ice cubes. She scooped some into a clean tea towel, wrapped them all up into a compress and said, "Here."

I pressed it to my sore cheek.

"Rennie, what are you going to tell your gran?" She bit her lower lip. She looked worried. It took me a second, but I got it. She was afraid I would tell on Derek. She was afraid I would get him into trouble.

"What do you want me to tell her?" I asked.

"I know you don't like Derek, and I can't say I blame you, the way he's been acting. He's not really like that, Rennie. But if Mr. Billingsley found out Derek hit a guest, he'd fire him immediately."

If she was trying to buy my silence, she was going about it the wrong way. Derek gone forever was a tantalizing thought.

"I was teasing Derek, but I love him, Rennie. We're working here for the rest of the season, and then we're heading east. Derek is going to get a job close to Harvard."

"Are you going to live together?" I knew it was none of my business, but I asked it anyway. I couldn't stop myself.

Annie laughed. "I may be American, but I'm not *that* American. I told him nothing doing until we're married."

"You're going to marry him?"

"I hope so. That's what I told my uncle."

I tried to hide how awful I felt. I was being as much of a jackass as Derek was. A different kind, but a jackass all the same. Annie was almost four years older than me. She had already graduated high school. She was so smart that she was going to be a doctor. What did any part of her life have to do with me? I'll tell you what. Nothing. Zero. Zilch.

"I guess I'll tell Grandma I fell." I looked at Annie to see if that was what she wanted.

She let out a whisper of a sigh. "Thanks, Rennie." She leaned over and kissed me on my good cheek. Then she reached for her big apron and those big yellow gauntlets of hers.

ELEVEN

I didn't go back into the dining room. Instead, I went outside to cool down. But just being outside wasn't enough. I needed to do something. I grabbed my skis and headed back to the slopes. I stayed out there for the rest of the day, until I was pretty much physically drained. But even that didn't get Annie out of my head.

I knew she was way beyond me, but it wasn't about that. I'd never met anyone like her. So smart. So confident. She knew exactly what she wanted, and I don't just mean Derek. She knew what she wanted to do with her life, and she had worked hard for the opportunity. If she kept working hard, her dream would come true. She was a million steps ahead of me. I felt like a big loser because I had no clue what I wanted besides not having to live with the Major anymore—not the way he was now, not after everything that had happened. I hadn't thought much about what I'd do after I left home. How was I going to support myself? What did I want to be? How did I want to spend the rest of my life?

The cop thing I'd told Annie? That's what I thought I wanted when I was a little kid, before I'd met a lot of cops. But now?

I planted my skis in front of the snack bar and nursed a hot chocolate. My face was swollen, and a pretty good bruise was developing. Grandma wasn't going to like this.

Someone did a throat-clearing "Ahem." I looked up and saw the guy from behind the counter standing at my table. He was wearing a parka and dandled a bunch of keys from one hand. I also noticed that it was dark outside and that we were the only two people in the place.

"Sorry," I mumbled. I grabbed my stuff and cleared out. I was heading for the back entrance to the chalet when I heard a voice. Raj's voice.

"Is this better? Can you hear me now?"

He sounded frustrated. He was standing near the equipment-rental place, holding a cell phone to his ear. I figured he was having trouble getting a signal. I stepped back a pace so he couldn't see me. Annie said she'd told him she planned to marry Derek. Maybe he was phoning home to break the news.

"Yes? Yes? am stuck in the mountains. In the snow." The way he said it, you'd think he was chin-deep in a steaming pile of manure. "No, no, everything is fine," he said. "There was a big storm."

That was news to me. We'd had a little snow, but nothing that would qualify as more than a flurry.

"It will be another day or two before the roads are clear enough for me to travel out of here," Raj continued.

What was he talking about? According to Rod, the roads into town were as clear as they ever were at this time of year.

Raj went on in a whiny voice. "But I assure you there is nothing to worry about. I will have the money. There will be no default." He was silent for a few seconds. "Three days at the most. I will be back in three days, and you will have the money. One way or another, you will have it. That is a guarantee."

Right. A guarantee from a guy who had just told a couple of whoppers. I remembered what Grandma had told me, that Raj had felt her out for an investment on their way from town to the resort. It sounded to me like Raj owed someone money. From the way he'd lied to explain why he hadn't coughed it up yet, I'd have been willing to bet it was a lot of money. On top of that, his mother-in-law, Annie's gran, was dying. Raj was not having a good year.

I heard Raj's voice again. "It is me. We must meet. Now."

He shoved his phone into his pocket and picked his way back to the chalet. With a sigh, I started to follow him. If Grandma wasn't back yet, she would be soon. One way or another, I was going to have to face her.

I saw Annie on the way to the stairs, but that's because I went out of my way to see her. She was clearly visible through the small round window in the kitchen door. She was swathed in her massive apron, her hair tied back and tucked under a white cap, and she was wearing the big yellow gloves that went all the way up to her elbows. She was standing on a metal step stool at a deep sink, scraping dishes, rinsing them and setting them into dishwasher racks. Clearly, she wasn't rushing off to meet her uncle.

I continued up the stairs and let myself into my room. Without turning on the light, I tapped softly on the door between Grandma's room and my own. There was no answer. I twisted the knob and nudged the door open. She was already asleep. I guessed getting around on crutches was more tiring than she'd expected. It meant a reprieve for me. I wouldn't have to explain anything to her tonight.

I stood at the window and saw someone walking up the driveway, away from the chalet. Raj. He was making his way to the road, still in those slippery city shoes of his that made getting a grip on the slope about as easy as grabbing hold of a greased pig, and if you don't know what I mean by that, then you don't have a grandma who grew up on a farm. With every step Raj took, one foot slipped backward, sending his arms pinwheeling as he tried to keep himself upright. I guess he didn't have much experience with snow.

I watched him, waiting for him to give up. Where did he think he was going anyway? There was nothing up there but more snow-covered gravel—for miles and miles. But he didn't quit. He kept inching his way closer to the top of the driveway. After a while he figured out that if he went up sideways, he could dig the uphill edge of his shoes into the snow, like you do when you go up a hill sideways on your skis. He wasn't any fun to watch after that. I undressed and got into bed. But I didn't stay there. I couldn't. My body wasn't ready to relax. Not even close.

I got up again and checked on Raj. He'd made it up to the road and was standing beside a truck, leaning into it. It looked to me like he was having a conversation with the driver. I hoped the poor guy wasn't asking for directions. Raj reached under his overcoat and pulled out something. I couldn't see what it was, but he handed it through the window to the driver of the truck. He stood there a little longer, talking—I guess, because his arms were flying out in all directions. A lot of people wave their arms around when they talk. Not a lot of people wave them around when they're listening to someone else talk.

Raj finally stepped away from the truck and watched from the side of the road while the driver turned to go back in the direction he'd come. I couldn't make out who Raj had been talking to, but the truck had a logo on the side of it. I could tell by its shape and by the splotch of its dark color against the truck body's light-colored paint job. After the truck had left, Raj started back down the hill. I stayed to watch and was glad I did. Those slippery shoes landed him on his butt three times before he made it to the bottom.

I looked from the window to my bed and knew there was no way I was going to be able to sleep. Not now anyway. I pulled on my jeans and T-shirt, got into my outdoor stuff and headed down the stairs and out into the night. Then I started to run. I thought maybe if I ran long enough, I'd be able to calm down. I had to. It's when I get all jazzed up, when I get antsy, that I end up in trouble.

There were a few paths around the chalet, and I ran on them. It was easy to put a circuit together. After that, it was just a matter of keeping my legs going and my breath as even as I could make it, concentrating on that, on my breathing and the rhythm of my legs. Just think about that, Rennie.

Don't think about anything else. Don't think about things you can't do anything about.

This was supposed to be the big thing I learned from Pete: Don't worry about the things you can't do anything about. Pete said it was a pretty simple idea, right? Well, duh. But it isn't just simple. It is blindingly obvious. It's why most people don't bother to vote, right? It's why they don't care about crime in someone else's neighborhood, but if something bad happens on their street or to someone they know, it is a different ball game. The world runs on people not thinking about the things they figure they can't do anything about, never mind worrying about them.

So don't think about Annie, I told myself. Don't worry about her. She has nothing to do with you.

And then, like a mirage or something, there she was.

I came around the corner and onto a stretch of path that ran parallel to the back of the chalet. I had a perfect view of the massive deck that was an outdoor restaurant during the day. One of the doors opened, and Annie stepped out into the pool of light thrown by the security light, which automatically turned on when someone came within range and stayed lit the whole time they were there. Her apron and yellow gloves were gone. So was the white cap, and she'd let her hair down. Her black hair flowed over her shoulders.

Someone stepped out of the shadows. Derek. Clearly, they'd made up. Clearly, they'd arranged to meet. Annie threw herself into his arms. Derek picked her up and twirled her around. Her laugh was like little bells.

I didn't feel like running anymore. I stayed in the shadows while I made my way back to the chalet. I didn't want Derek to see me. He'd never stop teasing me. Or maybe he'd get mad, saying I was stalking Annie or something. I had stepped back into the light when I heard a man's voice.

"Rennie? Is that you?"

It was Rod. He was standing in a doorway, but the door didn't lead into the chalet. What I mean is, it wasn't a door that guests used. Or staff, for that matter, unless they were looking for Rod. It turned out it was the outside door to his office.

He came toward me and took a good look at my face.

"What happened?"

"It was an accident." That was my story and I was going to stick to it, no matter what, for Annie.

Rod caught my chin in his hand and held it firmly when I tried to twist away.

"Unless I'm mistaken, it looks like you had a run-in with a fist." He finally let me go, and just in time too, because I started to get that feeling, the one that makes me tense up all over and signals my body to do something, do something *now*. "Puppy love. It can be a real bitch, am I right? Step inside, son. Let me see what I can do with that before your grandma gets a look at it."

The very last thing I wanted to do was step anywhere near old Rod. Or listen to him call me *son*. And I wanted to slug him for calling it *puppy love*. In the first place, he didn't know what he was talking about. In the second place, I know what they mean when they say puppy love. They mean it's cute. It's childish. *Aw, look at that, he's in love with someone twice his age.* Or ten years older. Or four.

They also mean that what you're feeling isn't real.

"Trust me, Rennie," Rod said when I didn't go inside with him. "You don't want Melanie to see you like that. She'll worry."

If I had to pick the one thing that made me do it, it was that last sentence. The thought of Grandma worrying about me made my stomach churn. It made me feel like I was going to throw up. I'd have done anything to avoid it, even follow Rod into his office.

TWELVE

Rod's office probably looked terrific during the day, when the light streamed through the windows that ran along two whole sides of it. The other two walls were covered with maps, charts and schedules. Rod turned on his desk lamp and twisted it up so that the light hit me in the face.

"I think I can do something with that," Rod said after another, shorter examination of my face. "Hang on. I'll be right back."

He disappeared through a door, and I heard him rummaging for something. I took a closer look around.

The maps were all of the same area—the Sierras around the chalet. One pinpointed all the ski runs, approved slopes, lifts and other ski resorts. Another was a topographical map that showed the elevations of the land. One map was covered with pushpins of different colors. They indicated places where there had been avalanches, and the different colors were for different years. A tiny strip of paper attached to each pin gave the date the avalanche had occurred. I noticed right away that some areas had seen plenty of avalanches, while in other places avalanches had occurred only once. Rod had it all tracked.

There were plenty of charts too. Staff duty charts, weather charts, planning charts, calendars marked up with different things that I guess Rod wanted to remember and hey, what do you know? A calendar that listed the upcoming avalanche-control blasts—when and where they were scheduled to happen. No wonder Rod was never surprised when a blast went off. He always knew when to expect one, right to the minute. I wondered if he got a kick out of seeing his guests jump when they heard an explosion. I probably would.

"Okay, take a seat, and let me see what I can do." Rod was back with a small basin, a washcloth that was wrapped around something—half a dozen ice cubes—and a jar of something else.

I sank into a leather armchair with a high back. Rod handed me the basin and the homemade ice pack.

"Hold that there for as long as you can stand it." He pulled up a chair. "You want to tell me what happened?"

No, I didn't. So I did what I always do when I don't want to talk about something. I shrugged and looked down, like I hadn't heard or didn't care or both. It drove the Major crazy and usually ended up with him yelling at me even louder than he had to start with. If there was anything that drove him crazy, it was a "who cares?" attitude, and I gave it to him pretty much every day.

Rod wasn't anything like the Major.

"I guess the real question is, what do *you* want me to do about it?" he said. "Keep that ice on there, son."

I prickled at the suggestion that I didn't know what I was doing.

"I can't have employees punching guests," Rod continued. "And I can't have guests knowing that something like this has happened—no matter how it happened or who did what or who started it."

Here we go. *No matter who did what or who started it.* It's what adults say when they want kids to confess to something, like the answer is black or white, yes or no, like anyone really knows who started it. Was it the kid who said something about the way my mom died? Or who asked an even dumber question, like, *Was she flattened*? Was it me when everything went black around that kid's head and my body took over from my brain and I hit him? Was it me because I was the one who begged Mom to take that side trip before we went home? Was it me because I nagged her and nagged her and nagged her?

It's not your fault. That's what they said every time I got into trouble because of some dumb kid with a dumb question. Or some jerk with a comment that made me want to knock all his teeth out. *It's not your fault what happened to your mother, Rennie. But you can't go around hitting people and getting into fights.* Because some kids fought back. If you ask me, some of them were picking a fight.

No matter who started it. Yeah, that really made me want to listen to whatever Rod had to say on the subject of *my* life.

"I was in love with a girl when I was about your age," he said. He was in the shadows, so it was hard to get a good look at him. Plus, he kept turning my head away from him so he could see the damage on my jaw. I, of course, had the light aimed right at me. I felt like a prisoner in one of those old cop movies, the ones that used to be in black and white before technology got hold of them. The cops are always in the shadows when they try to wring a confession out of their suspect,

133

and the guy being wrung out is always sitting in blinding light from the only lamp in the room. The heat from the lamp always makes him sweat too. "It was the same situation, which tells me that some things never change. She was a few years older than me. A real beauty—tall and athletic, not one of those prissy girls who never wants to chip her nails or muss her hair."

Like I said, I couldn't see his eyes. But I could hear his voice all right, and it was getting softer, and he slowed down a little, like he was enjoying what he was telling me. Or like he was remembering.

"She was nice to me, but in the way a big sister is nice to her kid brother. That's what I was to her. A kid. Even though, boy, my eyes just about popped out of my head every time I saw her. I was sure it was love."

"Yeah, but it wasn't. I get it." I threw the washcloth and ice into the basin and started to get up.

Rod tossed the jar to me.

"What's this?" There was no label on it.

"Take it with you. Put some on the bruise. It won't make it disappear, but it will make it look less serious. You might catch a break with your grandma."

It was worth a try.

"You want me to tell you who that girl was I had that crush on when I was your age?" Rod asked. He was leaning forward in his chair like he was dying for me to ask.

I shook my head. I didn't have to ask. I already had a pretty good idea.

THIRTEEN

You'd think a guy who ditched two whole weeks of school to run away to the ski slopes would be relaxed, right? He'd be having a good time. He'd be skiing and hanging out and sleeping as late as he wanted. Right? I know that's what I imagined when Grandma announced we were going skiing. But I couldn't sleep. Again. I felt like someone had dialed the world back nineteen months and I was me right after the accident. I couldn't sleep then either, not without seeing it—one minute we're cruising along this windy road blasted out of the rock that rises all around us. Mom is driving, and she's laughing and singing along to the radio. She loves that she decided at the last minute to rent a convertible. *I love the feel of the wind in my hair*, she says. She says it a couple of times. She knows the Major wouldn't approve. The Major is always fussing about safety and not taking risks. That means keeping her encased in the best that German engineering has to offer. He doesn't want her in a convertible any more than he wants her on a motorcycle. She knows it too. She keeps saying, *What would your father say?* and laughing.

The only constant is change—which means that nothing lasts forever. After one minute, there's another one. And that next minute changes everything.

Every time I closed my eyes for months after that, I saw it happen again, and every time, I woke up screaming. I felt like that now, only minus the screaming. I'd dozed off in the heavy armchair that I'd dragged over to the window. I'd probably dozed off a couple of times. What not only woke me but got me up out of the chair at dawn was an angry voice. Derek's angry voice. I *had* to look out the window. Maybe he and Annie were having a fight. Maybe they were breaking up.

Derek was down there, all right. But he wasn't yelling at Annie. At first I thought he was mad at the taxi driver, who was standing patiently beside his cab, watching Derek struggle to stuff a massive duffel bag and an equally large ski bag into the trunk and cursing when one fit and the other didn't. He pulled them both out and tried packing them at different angles. He was swearing and muttering the whole time. I knew because I pushed my window open so I could hear. Between the swearing, he kept saying, "Why didn't she tell me?"

The taxi driver finally stepped to the trunk and offered his help.

"I can do it," Derek snapped at him.

"If you want to catch your bus to Denver…" The driver's voice trailed off.

Denver? Derek was going to Denver? What was going on? Had he and Annie broken up?

But that didn't make sense, not after what Annie had said yesterday and what I had seen last night. Unless...had Annie agreed to go back to India with her uncle?

Derek stepped aside, gesturing elaborately at the gear he'd been trying to pack into the trunk.

"It's all yours, pal."

The taxi driver examined the cases and the available space before stowing the duffel bag effortlessly to one side of the trunk and sliding the ski bag in next to it. It was like watching Cinderella slipping her dainty feet into those glass slippers after her stepsisters had tried and failed to stuff their ugly dogs into them.

Derek looked back at the chalet. I ducked out of sight, but I could hear him just fine when he said, "I'll show her. I'll show her if it's the last thing I do."

The taxi door slammed, and when I peeked out again, the taxi was turning onto the road for town.

Derek, it seemed, was leaving Annie. But it didn't feel right.

I don't remember falling asleep after that. I don't remember dreaming either, but I must have been, and it must have been a good dream, because when I woke up, the sun was bright in the sky, and I was smiling. I'm not kidding. I could feel it. I had a great big grin on my face.

Then I remembered Derek and the taxi. He'd taken his ski gear with him, and the driver had said Derek had to catch a bus to Denver. Derek was gone. Maybe that's why I was smiling. But I still didn't get what had happened, and it still didn't feel right.

I turned over in bed and saw a note folded into a little tent on the bedside table. It was from Grandma. Rod was taking her for a drive to see the sights, and she hoped I would be able to amuse myself for the day.

I showered, changed and headed downstairs to get something to eat. I'd decided to take a look through that little round window into the kitchen and see how Annie was doing. Was she crying her eyes out over Derek like some girl in a chick flick?

Or was she glad he was gone? From what Derek had said, the breakup wasn't his idea. He was angry with her because she hadn't told him something. He'd threatened to get even with her. That had to mean Annie had changed her mind and dumped Derek, not the other way around. I hoped it was because she'd realized what a jerk he was. I worried that it was because she had agreed to go back to India with her uncle. But she'd had an argument with Raj too. She'd accused him of lying to her.

Annie wasn't in the kitchen. She was in the hall outside the kitchen, listening intently to what another woman was saying. The second woman was wearing an apron and a hairnet, so I guessed she worked in the kitchen with Annie. She pressed an envelope into Annie's hand. Annie frowned and opened it. She unfolded the piece of paper inside, read it and smiled. She tore off her apron, thrust it and her yellow gloves at the other woman and ran down the hall to the back door.

"What do you want me to tell Chef?" the woman called after her.

"Tell him I'm sick. Tell him I'm contagious. Tell him I died. I don't care. Derek has a surprise for me. He says I have to go and get it right now." She grinned and disappeared out the back door, leaving the other woman staring after her before casting a fearful look at the kitchen door. She gazed at the ceiling with her eyes closed, as if she was praying, drew in a deep breath and went inside.

I took off after Annie.

She had vanished by the time I burst through the door and into the yard. It had snowed again overnight, but a lot of people had been out already this morning, so the tangle of footprints was of no use to me. I ran up the steps to the deck to get a better view.

I couldn't see Annie from up there either.

Where was she? What kind of *surprise* had Derek left for her? Nothing nice, I was sure of that. Not the way he'd been talking a few hours ago. Whatever it was, he wasn't going to be around to take any blame for it. He was probably halfway to Denver by now.

What I didn't understand, though, was Annie's reaction to his note. She'd been happy when she read it. She'd been *thrilled*. All smiles. She'd been willing to face Chef's anger and punishment when she eventually went back to work. She'd raced off to find out what Derek's surprise was. In other words, she wasn't acting like someone who had just dumped him. She wasn't acting like someone who'd been dumped either. I got the same feeling I'd had before. It didn't feel right.

Then I spotted her. She'd put on her skis and was heading away from the chalet. Away from the main lifts too. Heading out-of-bounds.

Maybe it was Grandma's influence. Maybe it was what I'd read and heard about the dangers of being out-of-bounds. Or maybe it was just a case of the heebie-jeebies. All I knew was, what didn't feel right all of a sudden felt very wrong. Look at it, Rennie, I told myself. Add it up.

Derek took off in the middle of the night. He was angry. He swore he would *show her* even if it was the last thing he did.

The morning after he made his angry exit, Annie wasn't upset. Just the opposite. She was excited. She was happy. She couldn't wait to get her surprise from Derek. That meant (a) Annie didn't know Derek had left for Denver, and (b) she didn't know he was out to get her. Instead, she was acting like he was waiting for her somewhere so they could elope or something. She didn't know she might be headed for danger. And the only person I could think of who could warn her was me.

FOURTEEN

I raced back to the kitchen. A peek through the round window showed me that Chef Gaston was nowhere to be seen. I ducked inside and went straight for the woman who had given Annie the note.

"No, I do not know what it said," she said indignantly when I asked her if she knew what was in the note. "What do you think I am? A snoop? I found it and gave it to her, that's all."

"Do you have Annie's cell-phone number? It's important."

The woman, who up close didn't look all that much older than Annie, gave me a sour look.

"If she didn't give it to you, then I don't see why I should."

"It's important."

"Right." She started to turn away.

I grabbed her arm.

She plucked it off as if it were a worm.

"It's *really* important," I told her.

She rolled her eyes, dipped into the pocket of her apron and produced a phone, from which she read me Annie's number. I got out my own cell and punched in the number. Almost immediately the familiar strains of Annie's ringtone sounded behind me. I spun around. Annie hadn't magic-ally appeared, but a hoodie was hanging from a hook behind me, and the ringtone was coming from it. I dipped into the pocket. Sure enough, a cell phone. In her excitement, Annie had forgotten to take it with her.

I guessed I could have found someone to tell me how to reach Rod. Better, I could have called Grandma, and she would have passed her phone to Rod and I could have told him what was going on.

But what *was* going on? And even if I could convince Rod that something didn't smell right, what would he do? Call the cops? Where's the crime, Rennie?

I raced to gather my ski gear—all of it, including my avalanche gear, shovel, beacon and probe. I took my cell phone too, just in case.

It wasn't hard to track Annie. I'd seen the direction she'd gone in, and after last night's snowfall there was exactly one set of ski tracks going in that direction.

"Annie!" I cupped my hands around my mouth and shouted as loud as I could. "Annie!"

No answer.

She'd gotten a head start, and she was faster on skis than I was and in better shape too. I chased her until I was drenched in sweat and gasping like a dying man, but I couldn't catch up with her. Every time I had to stop to catch my breath, I knew she was getting farther and farther ahead of me.

I pushed on.

Up ahead, I saw a splotch of something moving.

"Annie!"

No answer.

I plunged forward and a few minutes later found myself plodding up a slope that Annie must have flown up. As I followed the curve of her path, I caught sight of something below. A building. The park ranger station. Annie had gone past it. Had the ranger seen her? If he had, he'd know how much of a lead she had on me. Maybe she'd even said where she was going or had asked for directions. I tucked my ski poles close and raced down to the station, executing a pretty sharp stop in front of the cabin just as a man stepped outside. It was Chuck Morrison, the ranger Rod had thrown out of his restaurant.

"Did you see a girl go through here not long ago?" I was breathing so hard I could barely get the words out.

"Girl?"

"On skis. She came down this way. There's her trail." I pointed.

"If you know that's her trail, why are you asking me if I saw her?"

"Did you? Did she say where she was going? Did she ask for directions?"

Chuck narrowed his eyes and took a long, suspicious look at me.

"What's going on here? Why are you so interested in the movements of this girl?"

I didn't have time for this.

"Never mind." I reached for my ski poles, which I'd planted in the snow. But Chuck grabbed my arm.

"Why are you following this girl? What's she to you? Are you stalking her?"

"Stalking? No!" Geez, don't start thinking now, Chuck. "I'm staying at Rod Billingsley's place with my grandmother. They're friends. You can check it out."

"That's what I intend to do, and you're not going anywhere until I do."

He confiscated my ski poles. I had no choice. I had to kick off my skis and follow him into the cabin.

"Can you at least hurry it up?" I asked. I should have known better. Asking guys in authority to speed up only makes them slow down, especially if they already don't like you or think you are up to something.

Chuck went behind a desk and started rooting around in a desk drawer for something. This was going to take *forever*. I glanced around. Maybe there were some poles in here somewhere that I could grab.

There weren't. The place was small and cramped, and that was with a grand total of one desk and one chair, plus one bookcase stuffed with bulging binders. Every bit of wall was covered with maps and charts and notices.

The one closest to me was the same avalanche map Rod had in his office and, next to it, the schedule of planned blasts. I hadn't studied it the night before when I was in Rod's office, but I looked at it now, mostly, I think, because I saw a red circle around today's date. A blast had been planned for late this afternoon. The time had been written in black marker. But the numbers in black had been crossed out with a red *X* and a new time written in, also in red. I glanced at the digital clock on the bookcase. The blast was scheduled for twenty minutes from now. I sure hoped it was nowhere around here.

That's when everything went cold, like I'd been touched by the King Midas of ice.

"Pike's Ride," I said to Chuck, who was still trying to get something out of the desk drawer. The way he was tugging at it and getting red in the face, the thing was stuck. "Where is that from here?"

He gave one last mighty tug and triumphantly held up a battered little book.

"Found it." He flipped through it until he found what he was looking for. "Pike's Ride? Why do you want to know that?"

"Just curious."

He looked me over again before nodding to the window behind him. My eyes followed. Through the window, out in the snow, I saw the twin grooves of a pair of skis.

Annie's ski tracks. I didn't want them to be hers. But when I traced the direction from which they had come, I knew they had to be hers. Who else could have made them?

I grabbed my ski poles from where Chuck had leaned them against his desk and made a dash for the door. My boots were clamped into my skis and my hand was in my pocket, rooting for my phone to call Grandma and get her to tell Rod to stop the blast, when Chuck exploded out of the cabin and threw himself at me in a low tackle. Geez, what was wrong with him? He was acting like I'd committed a capital crime and there was no way he was going to let me get away.

I fought back. You bet I did. But there was more to Chuck than met the eye. He practically ripped my jacket off me as he fought to keep me down. When he finally got me solidly pinned, he yelled at me that I wasn't going anywhere until he'd checked me out.

"You have to do something!" I screamed at him. "You have to stop that blast!"

He wasn't listening. Like every adult I'd ever met, he wasn't listening when it was important. That's what makes me see red. Then black. That's pretty much when I lose it, like I did then.

I stopped fighting him so hard. Let him think I was worn out. Or beat. When I felt his body start to relax, I brought up my knee as fast and as hard as I could. Ask me if I care if that was fighting dirty.

I took off while he was immobilized. By the time I had followed Annie's tracks to the top of a rise behind the ranger station, Chuck was struggling to his feet. I held my breath, willing him to do something to call off the blast. But he didn't rush back into the cabin, and he didn't pull out a phone. He wasn't going to do anything to save Annie. I would have to do it myself.

I dug into my jacket pocket for my phone to call Grandma and get Rod on the case.

My phone wasn't in the pocket.

It wasn't in any of my pockets.

I stared back at the cabin. It must have fallen out when I was wrestling with Chuck.

Finally, Chuck wheeled around and stumbled through the snow to the cabin. Maybe he was going to make the call and stop the blast, and maybe the best and safest thing for me to do was go back and wait for that to happen. Maybe.

And maybe not, because what's when I saw something I hadn't been able to see before—Chuck's ranger truck. It was parked behind the station. It looked an awful lot like the truck that Raj had met up on the road after his last argument with Annie.

I'd seen Raj at the ranger station the day before. Now it looked like Raj had called Chuck that night, and Chuck had come to meet him. They'd talked. But why? About what? What could they possibly have to talk about? Raj didn't know the first thing about skis and ski resorts. He'd come up here without a pair of boots. So why had he sought out a park ranger—at least twice? What possible use did Raj have for someone like that?

It hit me like a jackhammer to the belly.

FIFTEEN

Pop quiz: What does Chuck the park ranger do? According to Rod, at this time of year Chuck coordinates avalanche information and makes decisions about avalanche control.

That includes scheduling preventive blasts.

He's the guy in charge.

So Chuck must have been the one who had changed the time of the blast from late afternoon to—I swallowed hard—a time too close for Annie's comfort. What if he'd done that because Raj had asked him to? Because Raj had *paid* him to?

Rod had said Chuck would do anything for money. Raj had been sitting with us when Rod said it. He'd gotten a good look at Chuck. He knew where he was and what his job was, so it couldn't have been hard to find him. But why? Did he have a life insurance policy on Annie? Would he make a pile of money to pay off his debts if she died? Or was this an "honor" thing? She wouldn't do what he told her, so he was going to get rid of her?

Not that any of that mattered right then. The only thing that mattered was that Annie was headed for a blast zone.

I had to get to her. I had to do it *now*. I had to warn her. It was my only option.

It was Annie's only chance.

* * *

I don't think I've ever pushed myself as hard as I did in the next fifteen minutes. I dug my poles in and leaned hard on them to help power me on the uphill parts, and I tucked and planted myself in Annie's tracks going downhill. I ignored the sweat. I ignored the dryness in my throat and mouth. I told myself Annie mattered in a way that nothing else did. When I started to shake from exhaustion, from nerves, from being scared—I didn't know which and it didn't matter—I told myself that this time I knew it was coming. This time I had a choice. This time I wasn't just there. This time I could do something about it.

My lungs were tight. My legs were shaking. My arms were like jelly as I planted my ski poles again and again and drove my weight against them.

Finally I reached a crest that gave me a clear view of the slope ahead. There, skiing diagonally down and across it, was Annie.

I cupped my hands around my mouth and called her name, but I was drowned out by the *whoop-whoop* roar of a helicopter that at first I couldn't see.

I saw Annie turn her head, craning it toward the sound. If she just turned her head a little more…

"Annie! Annie!" I waved my arms. "Annie, he's going to blast!"

Her head swung around to face forward again. She hadn't seen me or heard me, and she didn't seem to think the helicopter posed any kind of a threat. For all I knew, they were a common sight up here, and not just because of the blasting.

I looked up again. Rotors appeared, whirring above the crest of Pike's Ride. I waved my arms above my head like an airport ground worker and prayed I could catch the pilot's eye.

Something flashed in the air near the copter.

The sky was blue above the pristine, sparkling white of the high slope. The air was still and clear. Annie was tracing a swath across the virgin snow. The sun warmed my upturned face. If you'd come across me in that split second, you'd have felt nothing but serenity. Tranquility. Peace.

In the next split second:

Ka-BOOM!!!

The air turned white. Visibility plummeted. I saw the mountain, and then I saw air filled with snow, rising instead of falling and pushing outward, farther and farther, snow as blast debris, snow propelled outward with the blast wave until Annie slicing across the slope was Annie half visible through a blizzard of snow before she disappeared completely in thickening clouds of white.

My heart slammed to a halt in my chest, and I couldn't breathe while I waited for the snow to settle. It seemed to take forever before the blanket of snow thinned to a fog and then to a mist. Suddenly the air was as clear as glass again. I stared out over the expanse of mountain where only a minute before I had been watching Annie describe a graceful downward swoop. Nothing was the same. Up near the top of the mountain I saw the crown of the slide—the place where a slab of snow had been jarred loose by the blast. I saw the slab's now-empty bed and, below that, the path the slab had taken as it shot downhill at 130 kilometers an hour, like a freight train, picking up more snow and ripping up, bowling over or burying everything in its path.

And at the bottom of the slope, I saw the runoff. The place where all that snow and all that debris had finally come to rest.

It was deathly silent.

There was no sign of Annie.

SIXTEEN

You'd think I would have sprung into action instantly, calling up every piece of information I knew about avalanches and rushing like a hero to Annie's rescue.

You'd be wrong.

I stood frozen to the spot where I'd stopped when the blast went off. I stared at the scene in front of me as it very slowly dawned on me that had I chased Annie even another three or four meters, there would be no sign of me either.

I started to shake. I was barely more than a couple of Rennie-lengths from having been swept away myself. Everything behind me was exactly the same as it had been when I skied across it. Everything in front of me was devastation. It was crazy how razor-thin the boundary was between the two, and it made me shake even harder to think it was a pure fluke that I happened to be on one side of the razor blade and not the other.

Unlike Annie.

"Annie! Annie!" I yelled her name over and over.

In return I heard the Major's voice. *Calme-toi, René. Tu ne peux pas penser si t'es pris de panique.* You can't think when you're freaking out, so calm down.

Fact: the majority of people who survive an avalanche either dig themselves out or have a piece of equipment or part of their body showing so that a rescuer spots them and digs them out.

As far as I could see, neither of these described Annie.

Only one in five people who are completely buried is ever rescued alive—and that's only if he or she is rescued quickly.

Time. It was all about time now. It was a race.

I patted myself down. I didn't have a cell phone, but I did have my avalanche pack and the three things that could help me most now: a transceiver, a collapsible probe and a collapsible shovel. I fumbled with the transceiver and almost dropped it, my hands were shaking so badly. I turned it to *Receive* and prayed that Annie had put hers on *Send* either when she set out or, if she'd had time, when she realized what was happening. I headed for the run off. My legs were jelly before I was halfway across. The area was huge. A minute had already ticked by. Maybe two. Or more. I had no idea how long I'd stood paralyzed by the thought that I could have been buried alive too.

Breathe, Rennie. Suck in a long, deep breath. Hold it. Now exhale. Slowly. And again.

Annie had been at least halfway across the slope that had avalanched. Halfway across and maybe halfway down. That, at least, gave me a start quadrant for my search. It also scared me, because the avalanche had come to rest at the bottom of the slope, which ended in a giant bowl-like depression. What if Annie had been swept into that bowl along with all the snow and whatever else the avalanche had picked up as it hurtled down the mountainside, the force and the volume of it more like a barrage of cold, wet cement than a flurry of snow? There'd been nothing lacy or frilly or Christmas-card-like about it. If Annie had been swept into that depression, I would never find her.

Calm down.

You have to look for her *now*, Rennie. The clock is running. If you don't find her and dig her out, she'll die.

So calm down.

I crossed the ravaged landscape to where I was sure I had last seen her. If I was going to do this right, I had to be thorough. I decided on a grid search. Sticking to it was one of the hardest things I'd ever had to do. I picked up nothing. I wanted to run to a spot farther away to see if she was there. But if I did that, I risked heading in the wrong direction. I walked the grid.

I was never going to find her.

Maybe she'd forgotten her transceiver like she'd forgotten her phone.

Maybe she hadn't turned it on.

Maybe she hadn't had time to turn it on.

Stick to the plan, Rennie. Keep going.

Then I had it. A signal. A *bip* and an arrow on the display screen pointing me farther down and across the mountain's scarred face.

I saw it almost immediately, but it took me a few seconds to believe it.

Something was sticking up out of the snow.

A tree branch? No, too thin.

A twig? Too straight.

A probe?

My beacon was blipping like crazy, and the arrow was pointing right at the straight, black, stick-like thing that was poking up at least thirty centimeters above the surface of the snow.

"Annie!"

I threw off my pack and assembled my shovel, telling myself the whole time to focus, take a deep breath, *do not panic.*

I dug.

"Hold on, Annie. I'm coming."

I drove the blade of that shovel into the snow again and again. It was like trying to slice through concrete with a butter knife.

Don't panic, Rennie. Don't think. Just dig. The probe is there. Unless it's some crazy fluke, that means that Annie is down there. Dig.

My heart thundered. Sweat poured down my face and prickled my armpits. My breath was a fog in front of me, making it hard to see.

Dig. Dig. Dig.

I was down about half a meter. An avalanche probe, fully extended, could be over two meters.

Don't think.

Do not think, and for sure do not think the worst.

Dig.

A flash of red.

Not blood red. Hot-chick-lipstick red. Cloth red.
Annie's jacket.

I threw myself down and started clawing at it.
"Annie! Annie!"

Hair. I uncovered a hank of her hair. Her head
moved.

She was alive!

"Annie!" I clawed out the snow around her.

She looked up at me, dazed but breathing.

"Are you okay? Is anything broken? Sorry.
Sorry. Dumb question. Just don't move, okay?
Just breathe, and I'll get you out of there."

She didn't move. She didn't say anything,
either, and one word flashed into my brain: shock.
That's when I did something I almost never do.
I said a silent thank-you to the Major. He was the
one who had enrolled me in a first-aid workshop,
and no amount of yelling or foot-stomping or
even wall-punching by me got me out of it.

These are things you should know, he'd insisted.
They are things everyone should know.

And don't you know it? Here I was, needing what I had learned that day but had resented having to learn.

I dug Annie out as fast as I could. I checked her over. It didn't seem like anything was broken.

"There was, like, an air bubble or something down there," Annie said, her voice low, her lips barely moving. I peeled off my jacket and wrapped it around her to fight the shock. "If there hadn't been…" Her voice trailed off.

I won't lie. The air was cold, and there was just enough breeze to whisk away whatever heat came off me, making me even colder. I had to move fast.

I looked around. I'd gotten Annie out of the snow, which was excellent, but there was no sign of her skis. She seemed mystified by their disappearance. We were a long way from the chalet, and far enough away from the ranger station, considering we had one pair of skis between us and I wasn't even sure how steady Annie was on her feet.

I was starting to shiver. I needed a plan. Now.

Start moving and keep moving was the only one that came to mind. I'd made it here from the ranger station in twenty minutes. If I could just make it back with Annie in the same time…

"Annie? Annie, do you think you can stand up?"

I got to my feet and put out my hands. She took them and let me help her to her feet. Her face was so white that it scared me. What if she had frostbite? What if something terrible was going to happen to her face even if I did manage to get her back to safety?

"We have to go back, Annie. We need to make sure you're okay."

She looked stiffly around.

"Derek," she said. "Where's Derek? He's supposed to be here. What if he got caught in the avalanche too?" A wild look came into her eyes. "Rennie, we have to find Derek!"

"It's okay, Annie," I said. "He's not here."

"But he's supposed to be here. He sent me a note."

"Derek left last night for Denver. I saw him go, Annie."

Annie didn't seem to understand. "Denver? But he asked me to meet him. He said he had something special he wanted to ask me. I thought…" She fell silent again.

"I don't know exactly what's going on, Annie. But we have to get out of here. Okay?"

She nodded.

"I'll go first and you follow me, okay? I'll do my best to make a trail." It would get easier, I hoped, when I reached the spot where I had stopped. From there I could retrace the path we had both already taken. I hoped Annie could move and keep moving. I hoped I didn't freeze to death. I hated being cold.

I also hated having to go first, but I had no choice. There was no way her boots were going to fit my bindings. With every step I took forward, I looked over my shoulder to make sure that Annie was following. She stayed behind me every step of the way, and pretty soon her face wasn't white anymore. Pretty soon it was pink. Then red.

She started talking after that. Or, to be totally accurate, she started asking questions. How come I had just happened to see the avalanche? Why had I been following her? What had I heard Derek say? What had I seen last night?

"Derek would never hurt me," she insisted. "Never."

"But I heard him, Annie."

She refused to believe it. "He would never hurt me, Rennie. This must all be a huge mix-up."

"The note Derek left for you—was it in his handwriting, Annie?"

"Derek's handwriting is illegible. He always texts me." She paused and looked at me. "Derek would never leave me a note. I don't know why I didn't think of that. He would have texted me. He always texted me."

"Was the note handwritten?"

"It was from a printer." She shook her head again. "I can't believe I didn't think of that."

"Do you still have it?"

"It's back in my room."

"If I'm right, I think someone left a note for Derek too. One that made him think you'd changed your mind."

"Uncle Raj." Annie looked like one of those superhero villainesses, ready to wreak vengeance on the world.

"Uncle Raj must be behind this."

"But why?" I asked.

"This has nothing to do with my grandmother," Annie said grimly. "There's nothing wrong with my grandmother. I talked to her. He said she was in the hospital and refused to tell me where. But I did what you said, Rennie. I called one of her neighbors. My gran isn't in the hospital. She isn't even sick. My uncle lied to me."

"Then why did he come here? What does he want? And why is he trying to kill you?"

"He came here to take me home so he could marry me off," she said. "To that nephew of his, one of his sister's sons. Uncle Raj raised him.

He'll do anything Uncle Raj wants him to, including marry me and let Uncle Raj continue to control the trust fund."

"Trust fund?"

"My father left me well provided for. My uncle has been controlling the fund. But he can't touch the money himself, except for an administrator's fee. When I turn twenty-one or when I marry, whichever comes first, the whole fund reverts to me. He probably wants me to marry Nirmal so he can get Nirmal to let him have complete access to the money."

"He can't force you to marry him, can he?" That wasn't possible, was it?

"You don't know what it's like in some places, Rennie. If I'd believed Uncle Raj about my gran and gone back with him, he would have taken me to his village, taken my passport away and married me off whether I wanted it or not. Then I would be no better than a prisoner. It happens, Rennie."

"What are you going to do, Annie?"

She shook her head, and we plodded on.

We slowed down when we approached the ranger station. Chuck's truck was gone, but still we proceeded with caution. The place was deserted, and the station was locked. I felt bad about what I did next, but I didn't think I had much choice. I needed to make a phone call.

"We should get back to the chalet before my uncle gets away," Annie said.

I broke a window in the ranger station so that we could get inside.

"Did you hear me, Rennie?"

"If you go back there without proof, your uncle will deny everything. He'll probably deny everything anyway."

I went to the wall where the blast schedule was posted and removed the thumbtacks holding it there. I folded it and slid it into my pocket.

"I also have to make a phone call," I said.

"Who are you going to call?"

Who else *would* I call?

I called Grandma.

SEVENTEEN

By the time I reached Grandma, Chef Gaston had already called Rod twice, first to complain that Annie had blown off her morning shift and again when she didn't show up for her lunch shift. Rod had followed up by calling Derek at the chalet, only to find that he was gone too. Then Chef called back to say that someone who claimed to be Annie's uncle was demanding to know what had happened to Annie and wanted to report her missing and was furious because the police told him they didn't go chasing eighteen-year-olds who had been missing for less than twenty-four hours, never mind less than six.

"He's not wasting any time," Annie said sourly. "He wants me dead so that the money reverts to him."

It was torture to keep her from marching into the chalet to confront her uncle. Grandma said we should wait until the police arrived. She said Raj might do something rash if he was desperate enough. She said to wait in Rod's office for the cops. She said his door was always open.

When they finally showed up, one cop went into the chalet and the other one, called Jackson, came to the office. He made us repeat our story a couple of times. He still looked skeptical when we finished.

"Let's go see what your uncle has to say," Jackson said.

Did you ever read the book *The Adventures of Tom Sawyer*? Me neither. My grandma read it to me when she came to stay for a month, back when my mom was still alive. There's this part in it where Tom and his friend Huck listen in on their own funeral before they reveal that they're still alive. Well, what happened next was sort of like that.

We followed him down the hall and stopped outside another office. There were three people inside: Raj, Chuck, and another cop. The cop was facing us. Raj and Chuck had their backs to us. Raj was talking.

"I am telling you, this man *saw* my niece. He saw her ski straight into a place that was about to be exploded."

"A blast zone," Chuck explained helpfully. So not only had Chuck changed the time of the blast to suit Raj's plan, but he was also serving as the eyewitness who had seen Annie go toward the blast zone, so that there could be no doubt about what had happened to her when she never showed up again.

"I am so afraid for my niece," Raj said to Jackson's partner. "You must try to find her."

Nothing could have held Annie back any longer, not that anyone tried.

"Liar!" she screamed at her uncle. "Murderer!" She flew at him and started hitting him. It took both cops to pull her off him.

"Is this your niece, sir?" Jackson's partner asked Raj with a straight face.

Chuck tried to weasel out of any wrong-doing. He said he'd told Rod about the change in the blast time and it wasn't his fault if Rod didn't keep his information up-to-date. He said he'd tried to warn Annie too, but she hadn't listened to him. He denied seeing me at all, even when I produced the updated blast schedule from his office. As for Raj, the notes to both Annie and Derek had been printed on stationery with a chalet watermark in it, and the woman on the desk the previous night said she had allowed Annie's uncle to use the printer. His cell phone was confiscated so that the police could follow up on the call I'd heard him make.

That was the breaking point for Raj. He fell to his knees and begged Annie for forgiveness. He begged her for the money too.

"These men who are harassing me—you don't understand, Annie. They started out as my business partners, but they turned out to be crooks. If I don't give them what they ask for, there's no telling what they'll do. Think of your auntie. Think of your grandmother. Please, Annie."

Some of the stiffness went out of Annie.

"I would never let anything happen to Auntie or Gran," she said. "But I'm not helping you, Uncle Raj. Not after what you did."

The cops arrested Raj and Chuck. Annie tracked down Derek, who was at the Denver airport, waiting to stop her from boarding a plane to India. The note he'd received said that Annie had agreed to go with her uncle because it was the right thing to do and that he should never try to contact her again. What Derek had set out to show her was that he loved her and would do anything to stop her from leaving him. It hadn't been a threat at all.

* * *

"My, don't you look handsome!" Grandma declared later that day.

I looked down at myself. I wasn't wearing anything special. Just a pair of black jeans and a brand-new shirt that Grandma had bought for me earlier when she was sightseeing with Rod.

Grandma was looking pretty good too. She was wearing a dress and one high-heeled shoe. She smelled like flowers. Rod was taking us out for dinner in town. I didn't want to go, but Grandma insisted.

"He's grateful for what you did," she said. "Think what would have happened if you hadn't sprung into action like that, Rennie. I'm sure Annie is asking herself the same question." I wished I was going out to dinner with Annie instead. "I'm so proud of you, Rennie."

I wondered if the Major would be as proud, assuming we ever got around to telling him how we had spent the time he was away.

Grandma's cell phone buzzed.

"Hand that to me, will you, dear?" Grandma asked.

I picked up her phone. The caller ID read *DM*, and when Grandma saw it, she shooed me out of the room, saying she had to take this and that it was personal.

"So who's DM?" I asked her later when I was helping her down the stairs to meet Rod.

Grandma smiled one of her mysterious smiles. "A friend," Grandma said. "An old friend."

"As in old boyfriend?" Grandma seemed to have lots of those kicking around. And she was still friends with most of them.

"You ask too many questions, Rennie. Now help me up. We don't want to keep Rod waiting."

It took us longer than usual to get downstairs. It turned out the combination of one foot in a cast and the other in a high-heeled shoe makes for tricky walking. But Grandma refused to change. She is like that. She always does things her way. It was what I like best about her.

NORAH McCLINTOCK writes mystery and crime fiction for young adult readers. She is the author of the Chloe and Levesque, Mike and Riel, Robyn Hunter, and Ryan Dooley series, as well as many stand-alone novels. Norah grew up in Montreal, Quebec, and lives in Toronto, Ontario. She is a five-time winner of the Crime Writers of Canada's Arthur Ellis Award for Best Juvenile Crime Novel. Her novels have been translated into sixteen languages. For more information, visit www.norahmcclintock.com. *Slide* is the prequel to *Close to the Heel*, Norah's novel in Seven (the series).

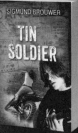